PURE SPRING

BRIAN DOYLE

Pure Spring

GROUNDWOOD BOOKS
HOUSE OF ANANSI PRESS
TORONTO   BERKELEY

Groundwood Books / House of Anansi Press
110 Spadina Avenue, Suite 801, Toronto, Ontario M5V 2K4

Distributed in the USA by Publishers Group West
1700 Fourth Street, Berkeley, CA 94710

We acknowledge for their financial support of our publishing program the Canada Council for the Arts, the Government of Canada through the Book Publishing Industry Development Program (BPIDP) and the Ontario Arts Council.

ONTARIO ARTS COUNCIL
CONSEIL DES ARTS DE L'ONTARIO

Library and Archives Canada Cataloguing in Publication
Doyle, Brian
Pure Spring / by Brian Doyle.
ISBN-13: 978-0-88899-774-6 (bound). – ISBN-10: 0-88899-774-4 (bound).
ISBN-13: 0-88899-775-3 (pbk.) – ISBN-10: 0-88899-775-2 (pbk.)
1. Pure Spring Company – Juvenile fiction.
I. Title.
PS8557.O87P87 2007   jC813'.54   C2006-905940-3

Cover photography by Tim Fuller
Design by Michael Solomon
Printed and bound in Canada

To Shelley Tanaka

Like all great editors, she can make
just about anybody look good.

Contents

1

Dump the Lie

"Name?"

"Martin."

"Gotta last name?"

"O'Boy."

"O'Boy?"

"O'Boy. Martin O'Boy."

"People call you Boy? Boy O'Boy?"

"Sometimes. But I don't like it."

"You don't like it?"

"No. No, I don't." Am I being rude?

"Why? Why don't you like it? It's a nickname. All kids should have nicknames. I always wanted a nickname when I was young. But nobody would tag one on me. Come over here…"

If he asks me again I can tell him that I don't like it because I think they're making fun when they call me that.

He's got a nice face, Mr. Mirsky has. Kind, soft eyes, large nose and forehead. Granny always used to say that a large forehead showed you were very smart. Lots of brains in there, lots of room…

I go around the desk where he's sitting and he stands up. He puts his hands on my shoulders and then he squeezes my arms.

"You're big enough. Should be strong enough to lift crates of soft drinks on to a truck. Why did you come to Pure Spring for a job?"

Funny, but I don't feel very big. Not big at all. Small, in fact.

"I like the trucks. The shape of them. The color. And I like the drinks. Specially Honee Orange."

He likes what I just said. His eyes are smiling now. He's proud.

"Now, you have to be sixteen years of age. Are you sixteen? It's against the law for me to hire people who are under sixteen. You don't want to get me in trouble, do you?"

"No, sir."

"Well? Are you sixteen or over? What's the answer?"

My dead granny told me never to lie. Lying poisons your soul, she said. She also told me that I was too beautiful to be a boy and my curly blond hair and large blue eyes will be a curse I'll have to live with the rest of my life.

But now I'm going to lie. I'm not sixteen. I only maybe look sixteen because I'm big for my age and I guess I'm pretty strong. I have my birth certificate right here in my wallet in my pocket.

I put my hand in my pocket and hold on to my wallet.

I don't want my birth certificate to jump out on to Mr. Mirsky's desk while I'm telling my lie.

Grampa Rip got me this pocket-sized birth certificate when I first came to live with him. He said that if ever I forgot who I was all I had to do was look in my wallet and there the answer would be.

He knew that sometimes I'd get so scared I'd lose myself and I'd become nobody, a blank.

Me and my cat Cheap live with Grampa Rip. Cheap has only one ear. My father bought him for ten cents for my birthday a few years ago as a joke. Ten cents. Cheap. Really funny.

Well, he won't be making jokes like that any more. Or any kind of jokes.

Grampa Rip is pretty smart sometimes. Especially when he got all the information about me and got me my birth certificate. Very smart. But sometimes his brain goes away — far, far away — and he's not smart any more. That's when I have to take care of him. Make sure he's all right. Our old neighbor, my hero Buz Sawyer, suggested that I go and live with his grandfather Rip Sawyer for two reasons. One, so's I'd have a place to live, and two, so's I could take care of Grampa Rip when his mind went away.

Back to Granny again.

She also told me that people want to believe somebody who has a beautiful face. That's why some movie actors can tell you anything and you'll believe it.

"What's the answer?" Mr. Mirsky says.

I dump the lie into his kind face.

"Yes," I lie, "I'm sixteen."

"When is your birthday?"

"When they dropped the atomic bomb and killed all the people. August 6."

He's looking at me.

"You didn't take that personally, did you? The bomb. All the people who died?"

"I hated it," I say.

"So you'll be seventeen on August 6," he says.

I don't answer. Is silence a lie, too?

I know he likes me. I don't let the shame of my lie show in my shameful eyes.

He blinks his kind eyes. "I don't suppose you have any proof of age with you? Birth certificate or something?"

"No, sir," I lie again, squeezing my wallet, squeezing it until it bends in my pocket. Squeezing my name, my date of birth. Squeezing myself.

"No, I didn't think so. Hardly anybody has that kind of proof at your age...I think you are honest, Martin O'Boy. You're hired, hired as a helper. You know, we're honest here at Pure Spring, too. We are a trusted company. We are a proud company. We have good relationships with our customers in the Ottawa area. And our drivers are honest. They don't steal from the customers. And our helpers, too. They are honest. Like you, Martin O'Boy. You will be a helper. You, of course, will not steal drinks to drink free from the truck.

"We have, though, I should tell you, a special privilege for a helper that even the driver doesn't have. The helper

14

may have *one* free drink of his choice. You'll probably choose Honee Orange to drink, to wash down your lunch. I see you have your lunch with you. That brown bag?"

"Yes. That's my lunch."

"And may I ask, my young friend, who made that lunch for you?"

"I made it."

"Your mother didn't make it?"

"No, sir."

"Your father, then?"

"No, sir. Not my father."

"Who, then? Who do you live with?"

"Grampa Rip."

"Is he your mother's father, Grampa Rip? Or is he your father's father?"

"He's Buz's grandfather."

"Who's Buz?"

"My hero neighbor. He's gone back to war again. In Korea this time. The Korean War. He's a pilot. He flies airplanes. He's my hero."

"Wait a minute. Grampa Rip. Is his last name Sawyer? Rip Sawyer?"

"Yes."

"I know him. I know Rip Sawyer. A fine and cultured gentleman. He used to work for my father when he first started this business. Took care of my father's horses, wagons and sleighs. Ottawa. Everybody knows everybody in Ottawa and the Ottawa Valley. Wonderful thing, that!"

"Yes, sir," I say.

"I guess you don't go to school. It's April 1. School isn't out until June."

"No, I don't go to school."

"Did you quit school?"

"Sort of."

"Why did you quit?"

"I couldn't go."

"Why?"

"Because I got sick."

"Where are your parents?"

"I don't know."

"You don't know?"

"No."

"Why?"

"Something happened."

What Happened • One

*Y*OU WERE *up to your father's shoulder now. He
said you were growing like a weed. You didn't like
it when he said that. A weed. You didn't like anything
your father said. A weed is a thing you don't want.
That you don't like. It's something you pull out by the
roots and throw out of the garden because it's sucking
all the good things that the good plants in the garden
want.*

*"Don't be so touchy," your father said. "It's just an
expression. Unless you think you* are *a weed. If you are,
then you could pull yourself out of the garden and toss
yourself over the fence right now!"*

*Your granny always told you to pay attention to peo-
ple's words, the way they choose to say things. The words
that people say can show a lot about those people. You can
find out a lot that way. A lot about what they think. A
lot about what they don't say with their tongues out loud*

but they say inside with their brains. Behind the words they say out loud.

You looked at the scar between his eyes while you were discussing weeds.

The time he was full of beer and was shaking your twin brother Phil to get him to stop howling and your mother was shrieking and Phil's head was going to fly off and you picked the ketchup bottle off the table and hit your father right between the eyes with it.

You threw it as hard as you could, like you'd throw a baseball. The bottle turned in the air once and then the heavy bottom of it hit him square between the eyes.

The blood spurted straight out of your father's fore-head like the stream you see in pictures of those fountains where they have the statues of those cute little boys pissing up and over and down in a nice rainbow arc.

The glass in those ketchup bottles is very thick and that ketchup bottle was very heavy.

Your father stumbled into the kitchen and after a while came back, silent, with a blood-soaked towel around his head.

Your mother took your twin brother Phil, who was not like you at all and was still howling and struggling, upstairs.

Your father, from under the bloody towel, said, "If you ever do anything like that again, I'll kill you!"

He never once mentioned it after that. And neither did you nor anybody else. But the scar was there to remind everybody every minute, every hour, every day. Every day he shaved he saw it in the mirror.

Every time he looked at you he saw the scar in the mirror of your eyes.

2

How to Know Grampa Rip

I'M SITTING on a park bench right across the street from where we live, Grampa Rip and I — 511 Somerset Street West, Apartment 4.

There's still some snow on the ground but it's a warm spring day.

There's a gray man in a gray raincoat and a gray hat sitting two benches down. Across and down the street outside Smitty's Smoke Shop, Smitty is washing the winter off his window. On the right side of the park, in front of St. Elijah's Antiochian Orthodox Church, the priest is walking up and down in the spring sun squinting at his holy book. Nobody else around.

While I was talking to Mr. Mirsky at Pure Spring this morning, Mr. Mirsky's secretary, Anita, came in and told him he was wanted on the phone. He told her to give me an application form to fill out and then he told me I couldn't start work today because the drink truck was already gone out and that I should come to work tomorrow at 7:00 A.M. in the morning and start to work.

Anita was shorter than I am, even with the high heels she had on. She was wearing a tight red skirt and a frilly white blouse and lots of lipstick and perfume. She waved her eyelashes at me and then got me an application form and sat me down at a table and gave me a pen.

"Fill this out and leave it with me and come in a little before 7:00 A.M. in the morning tomorrow and you'll be with Randy in truck number 15," Anita said.

"Randy?" I said.

"Right choo are!" she said. "Randy!"

"Truck 15. Randy," I said.

"Right choo are!" she said. And then she said, "And God help ya!"

Grampa Rip's not home. He's at McEvoy's Funeral Home on Kent Street near St. Patrick's Church. Every day (well, nearly every day) Grampa Rip gets all dressed up — long-sleeved white shirt, vest, watch and chain, suit jacket, nice pressed pants to match, tie and black fedora hat — and off to the funeral home he goes for most of the afternoon.

I was friends with Grampa Rip before I went to live with him. My hero, Buz Sawyer, asked me once if I wanted to go and help him move his grampa from his nice house on Bayswater Avenue to an apartment or rooms somewhere because his wife had died and left everything to the Catholic Church — the house, all the money, most of the fancy furniture, everything — and so Grampa Rip was all of a sudden kind of poor and kicked out of where he was living.

My friend Billy Batson and I went with Buz in his convertible car to help his Grampa Rip Sawyer move.

The moving truck was called Bye Bye Moving. And written underneath in smaller letters it said *Let someone who cares handle your valuables.*

"They won't be handling my valuables," said Grampa Rip, "but they can move the furniture!" Buz laughed his head off and I laughed, too, and Billy Batson whispered to me what's so funny and I told him that when Grampa Rip said "my valuables" he meant what's hanging between his legs.

"SHAZAM!" said Billy Batson.

Billy Batson made me laugh. He had the same name as the boy in the comic books who can change into Captain Marvel.

In the comics, a homeless orphan called Billy Batson meets a wizard who gives him a magic word to say. The word is SHAZAM!

The homeless orphan Billy Batson says SHAZAM! and then there's a picture that says BOOM! and Billy changes into Captain Marvel who looks a lot like Fred MacMurray, the movie star, except for his clothes. Captain Marvel has a tight red suit on with a yellow belt, yellow cuffs, yellow boots and a white cape with yellow trim.

And on his chest is a yellow lightning bolt.

When my friend Billy got excited about something he'd

say the word SHAZAM! and shut his eyes and wait. Then, he said, his brain would swell up like Captain Marvel's chest.

Here's some of the stuff Grampa Rip had for us to move: the kitchen table with the huge wooden legs carved like giant bowling pins (takes two strong men to carry it); four heavy high-backed oak chairs with lions carved on the two back posts; a large brass bed; an enormous rocking chair with wooden eagles on the posts; a monster desk, higher than I can reach, with glass doors, a rolltop cover, eight drawers and dozens of cubbyholes with four differ-ent keys to lock the different doors and compartments (Grampa Rip calls it his secretariat — a small person could *live* in this desk); two very heavy high brass floor lamps with tassels hanging from the shades; three giant holy pic-tures with massive wood frames — one of Jesus' head wearing his crown of thorns with drops of blood on his forehead, his eyes turned up to heaven, another of the Pieta, the Virgin Mary, dressed in blue, with the dead body of Jesus on her lap, and another one of Jesus carrying his cross which is about the size of one of Grampa Rip's holy pictures through a crowd of spectators (one of these pic-tures could cover more than half a wall); a massive strong-box about the size of a small bed with iron reinforced cor-ners and hinges big enough for Hercules and an ugly big padlock that weighs as much as a large rock (this box is always locked and weighs a ton).

The place we moved Grampa Rip to that time was a garage made over to be a kind of one-room house. It was in the backyard of a house near Glebe Collegiate on a pretty rich street, Clemow Avenue. The lady was a friend of Grampa Rip's dead wife. You could tell Grampa didn't like her very much. She was standing on her back veranda telling the moving guys who came with the Bye Bye Moving truck to be careful with their truck backing it up.

"Look at the mouth on her," Grampa Rip said. Her mouth was just a slit and she didn't seem to have any lips. "I wonder how she feeds herself…got a face on her like a mud pout…"

I wondered how — after we got all his stuff stuffed in the garage — there was going to be any room for Grampa Rip. How could he live here if there was hardly any room for his own self?

A few days later Buz told me his grampa was moving again but he couldn't help him this time because he was getting ready to go to Korea to maybe be a war hero and Billy Batson himself had moved out of Lowertown the day before and could I go over and help Grampa Rip.

When I got there the moving guys had most of his stuff back in the truck and Grampa Rip was having an argument with the Mud Pout about a lamp that was missing. Two of Grampa Rip's huge brass floor lamps were stored in her basement because there was no room in the garage for them, but only one lamp came out of the basement.

"Where's the second lamp?" Grampa was saying. "There were two lamps down there."

"No," she was saying,"You're losing your marbles, Rip. There was only *one* lamp stored down there…"

The moving guys, Frankie and Johnny, were standing there listening, their arms folded across their chests, their muscles bulging, smiling a little bit to themselves, wondering what was going to happen with Grampa Rip's lamp.

After Grampa and the Mud Pout argued back and forward for a while, Grampa suddenly says this: "All right then. Here's what we'll do. We'll be pullin' out now. I'm moving into a decent place, and in the meantime you can take that brass floor lamp that you're after just stealing from me in front of these witnesses here in broad daylight and you can shove it as far as it will go right up you know where!"

Frankie and Johnny were holding their sides laughing.

Then Grampa and I got on a streetcar and met the Bye Bye Moving truck over at his new place.

On the streetcar Grampa said, "That's the way *my* grampa, Grampa Hack Sawyer, used to talk. Crude but effective."

The new place had two rooms and a sink and toilet at the back of an old house on Preston Street not too far from where I was this morning at the Pure Spring Bottling Company on Aberdeen Street.

By the time Frankie and Johnny got most of Grampa's stuff into the rooms there was a little crowd of neighbors watching. By the time they wheeled Grampa's secretariat down the laneway on a dolly the crowd was oohing and ahing. They were very excited about the size of Grampa Rip's furniture.

When we carried the holy pictures past there was some clapping.

It took the four of us to lift the strongbox.

"What've ya got in here, Mr. Sawyer?" says Johnny.

"Wouldn't you like to know, eh?" says Grampa Rip and gives me a wink.

But when we set down the box, the floor suddenly started to creak and we just got out the door in time, when the whole room caved in.

Grampa Rip had to go and stay at the YMCA for a while until he found another place. And he did find one.

And I was helping once again. Getting to know him.

"How much would you say one of these pictures weighs?" says Frankie as he and Johnny carried Jesus and his thorns up to the third floor of an apartment on King Edward Avenue near the synagogue.

"I hope you can stay here in this one," I said to Grampa Rip. I said that because of the two long rows of beautiful elm trees that could be so pretty in the winter and so cool making shade in the summer. What a beautiful street King Edward Avenue is! What a boulevard!

Because the staircase was so narrow the secretariat got stuck and Frankie and Johnny had to take the banister off to get the big desk down again.

They were shaking their heads.

Maybe the Bye Bye Moving company would like to say bye bye to Grampa Rip.

They got the secretariat back outside.

They rigged a pulley on the balcony of the third floor

and tried to pull her up with ropes but the pulley gave way and the whole thing crashed back down on the lawn. The secretariat now had a big crack in it.

"You'll have to put this monster in storage, Mr. Sawyer," says Frankie, or was it Johnny.

"I'm not living without my secretariat," says Grampa Rip.

And so on to the next place a week or so later.

"We're sure gettin' to know your stuff real well, Mr. Sawyer," says Frankie while we're bolting together the brass bed in Grampa's new place on York Street near York Street School.

"I wonder," says Johnny, "how the lady over at Clemow Avenue is doing tryin' to put that brass lamp up where Mr. Sawyer told her to put it!"

But when the landlord looked at Grampa's stuff coming out of the Bye Bye Moving truck *(Let someone who cares handle your valuables)*, especially the three holy pictures, he didn't like it and changed his mind about Grampa.

"What's the trouble, Mr. Applebaum?" says Grampa.

"We don't go for that voodoo around here," says Mr. Applebaum, "and anyway I forgot to tell you, the place is taken. I got some relatives from Poland coming."

At last Grampa came here, Somerset Street, right across from where I'm sitting eating my roast pork and hot mustard sandwiches.

And now I'm living here with him.

He's really good to me. And I'm good to him.

I think, maybe, we love each other.

Dundonald Park is the name of the park I'm sitting in. The air is a bit chilly but the sun is warm on me. There are still patches of snow on the ground but there's grass showing. The trees have no buds yet but if you look at a whole tree, not just the branches and twigs, it looks like any minute now it's going to start to explode in slow motion with buds.

There's a robin. Is it a boy robin or a girl robin? Boys. Girls. Soon he'll, she'll pull a big fat worm out of the grass but not yet. He makes, she makes a beautiful sound like fat water dripping. Velvet.

There's Billy Finbarr, our paper boy, home from school for lunch. He gives me a wave. This afternoon he'll pick up his papers and fold each one into a tight roll, a "biscuit," so he can go around his route and throw the papers at the houses from his bicycle.

At our apartment, though, he can't do that. He has to bring the paper upstairs and then throw it as hard as he can at our door. When we hear the thump, we know what it is. It's our paper.

There's part of the Ottawa *Evening Journal* newspaper on the bench beside me. It's open. There's an ad.

Toni Home Permanent
Which girl has the natural curl
And which girl has the TONI?

There's a picture of two girls. Which one?

A beautiful girl walks past on Somerset Street. I feel like shouting to her, "Are you the girl with the NATURAL CURL or are you the one with the TONI!"

But I wouldn't dare.

The Gray Man looks at her, too.

I see, across the street in our round bathroom window, Cheap, my cat. The four bathroom windows in our apartment building are all round like the portholes of a ship. I'll go over soon as I'm done this pork and hot mustard sandwich and get Cheap and take him for a ride on my bike. He likes to get in the basket. Sticks his face right into the wind. Thinks he's a dog. He'll get a snootful of spring air!

Underneath the Toni Home Permanent ad in the paper there's a beautiful picture of the movie star Esther Williams. She's in a new movie about bathing suits. She has very long legs. She's standing on her toes.

There's a lady with her kid walking up Somerset Street. She is giving the kid a candy. The candy falls in the dirt. The lady picks it up, licks off the dirt, gives it back to the kid's mouth. The kid, like a baby bird in a nest, opens up and in pops the candy, *Chirp! Chirp!* The Gray Man watches, too. Then he picks up his paper and reads. He looks up often over the paper.

Can Cheap see the Gray Man from his porthole window where he loves to sit?

I'm thinking about this morning. Mr. Mirsky's honest eyes. The lie I dumped in. And then Anita. All the lipstick and the perfume. And what she said. Randy, she said. Truck 15. Seven A.M. in the morning. Right choo are!

And then, "God help ya!"
God help ya? What did she mean by that?
Anyway. We'll soon find out.
Here I come, Cheap. Look out! I'm very happy!
I've got a job!

3

Rising to Gerty

"Seven a.m. *in* the morning," Grampa Rip is say-ing. "It's redundant to say *in the morning* if you say A.M. A.M. *means* morning! It's Latin. Ante meridiem. Ante, *before.* Meri, *middle.* Diem, *day.* Same as P.M. Latin! P for post meaning *after.* Meridiem, midday, noon. After noon! See? Easy, eh? A.M. P.M. Before noon. After noon. Twelve hours before noon. Half a day. Twelve hours after noon. Another half a day. Twenty-four hours in a day. And I'll tell you this! If the sun came up at noon and went down at midnight then those geniuses over at Pure Spring wouldn't be nearly so confused, now would they! Now, you better get a move on. You don't want to be late — get there at five minutes *after* 7:00 A.M. in the morning, now would you? And don't forget yer lunch!"

Grampa Rip's smart. But sometimes he tells you too much. He loves words. He loves language. He loves books. He loves life.

I take the Somerset streetcar and transfer at Preston

Street. It's raining misty rain. Where I get off the streetcar at the corner of Aberdeen and Preston there's an old Italian lady all dressed in black leaning way over on her little lawn squinting at a purple crocus flower peeking up out of the grass between some patches of snow.

In the big yard at the Pure Spring Company, 22 Aberdeen Street, there are about twenty trucks waiting with their engines running. There are men in maroon jackets and pants moving around the trucks, standing talking to each other, adjusting the cases of drinks on their huge trucks. Their caps are maroon, too. Their shirts are khaki colored. The black tie looks nice with the shirt.

The trucks are white and strong looking. The backs are open. I count the cases. Four rows ten cases long, five cases high. I'm good at math. The trucks hold two hundred cases each.

A black-and-white stripe along the side of the truck under the load says *Honee Orange*. On the door is the Pure Spring shield. The shield is black and gold. There's a gold crown on the top. Under the crown are four panels. In one is a drawing of a fountain. Then three goofy-looking lions. In the third, three fleurs de lys. In the fourth, a beautiful brown woman carrying a box on her shoulder.

She has no clothes on. Her breasts are in full bloom.

Under that, a crest, black and red. *Pure Spring Ginger Ale*. And under that it reads

Think Pure

I look back up at the shield, at the breasts. Look closer. Nipples.

"Think pure!" a voice behind me says. "Think pure!" Then laughs.

"You're O'Boy, right? My new helper? Truck 15's over here. We're almost ready to go. Here, put this on. I'm Randy."

Randy hands me a khaki shirt. It is just like his. It's got the Pure Spring shield on the pocket.

"That's the Pure Spring shield. See? There's fleurs de lys — we sell drinks to Frenchies. Lions — that's for the English. The fountain — well, that's the pure water of the spring. And the brown-skinned girl — she's carrying ginger in that box, ginger for the ginger ale, get it? But you weren't looking at the ginger box, were ya? That's only a picture, ya know. The real thing's lots better..."

I'm embarrassed. I get in the truck and put on the shirt.

It's time to go. There's a big roar, all the trucks' engines getting revved up. Out of the yard we go. Our truck, truck 15, leaves the gate. I see, at the gate, Mr. Mirsky standing, his arms folded, watching us all leave. He's proud of his fleet. His chin is up. His bald head almost glistens in the spring soft morning light. His face looks good on him. Proud. Like my shirt with the Pure Spring shield on the breast pocket. Looks good on me, I know it does.

"What we do — what's your first name, oh yeah, Martin, well, we'll have to do something about that — what we do is put our valuables in the glove box and lock it. Your wallet and stuff. There's lots of dishonest people out there, Martin — oh, we'll have to do something about that name — there's thieves and cheats and pickpockets and you'll be concentrating on your work in cellars and cramped places and you never know…"

I obey and take out my wallet and put it into the glove box and he locks it. I notice he doesn't put his own wallet in there. Maybe it's already there.

But doing it doesn't feel right.

Grampa Rip got me the birth certificate not too long after I went to live with him. Also the wallet to keep it in. He told me to swear to him I'd never lose it. He got very excited the way he gets sometimes. He said it's the most valuable document I'll ever own. Don't let it out of your sight. Don't let anybody ever touch it. It proves you're a Canadian, you were born here, best country in the world, everybody in the universe wishes they were a Canadian, you'll always be a somebody when you have that plasticized proof right in your wallet…always remember that…the envy of the world…a wallet-sized plasticized birth certificate…

Our first stop is McDowell's Grocery and Lunch on Sweetland Avenue in Sandy Hill.

Randy squeezes big number 15 into the little laneway.

"As soon as we go in, you'll go down the cellar and open the cellar window and throw out six cases of Pure Spring — six *full* cases of whatever he's got that's full down there. Then come right up."

I go down the steep, steep rickety wooden steps almost like a ladder into the dark, damp, musty, low-ceiling cellar. At first I can hardly see anything. Soon I see the light of the cellar window. I feel my way over and unlatch the window.

There are cases and crates and bottles full and empty and supplies piled up everywhere. I find four cases of ginger ale and two Honee Orange, full, and lift them out the little cellar window.

It feels good. I'm working! Getting paid!

I go back up. Climb back up.

Randy is talking to Mr. McDowell. He's a little old man leaning on a cane. He's thin. His cheekbones stick out. He's got brown spots on his hands. He's talking business with Randy. The price of this and that.

Mr. McDowell spits a gob of phlegm out of his throat into a pail in the corner. You can hear the green yellow gob clicking in his chest as he breathes and coughs.

"Did you get those *empties* out of there, Martin?" says Randy. "Good. Wait for me at the truck. How many empties, Martin? Six. Good. Okay. I'll go down and see what Mr. McDowell needs…"

I go outside. My head is spinning. Empties? Did I make a mistake? Didn't he say full ones?

Outside, Randy's throwing out from the cellar eight cases of empties and telling me to put them on the truck. Now I'm confused. But I do as I'm told.

When I'm finished, Randy comes to the door and says really loud, "Mr. McDowell needs eight full. Four Honee Orange and four ginger ale!"

Then he rushes past me and grabs two cases of Honee

Orange off the truck and puts them with the six cases that are already there. The ones I put out.

We've just sold Mr. McDowell six cases of his own full ones!

Then Randy bangs around for a while and tells me to go down the cellar again, tidy up the cases a bit, make some noise and then come up. I do that, what I'm told. Now it's time to go back up into the store.

Before I put my foot on the first steep step I look up. From the darkness I'm in into the light up there I see a swinging blue skirt, black small shoes with flashing silver buckles, curving graceful legs in silk stockings with wide blue garter tops, pale-blue panties with rose-pink-colored ribbon trim — a flashing sight, now gone.

I come slowly up the ladder.

My body is half into the store now.

I always dreamt, especially in the spring, that the girl of those dreams would appear up from down below — rise up, the floor or the earth *opening* up in my dream and she'd come up to where I was standing.

But now it's the opposite.

It's me rising.

I hear a happy little laugh. She's chatting with a customer. She's behind me at the counter. I shut the trap door to the cellar. Quiet.

I turn and look. She looks down at her shoes. Shy. She glances up. Then she pouts pretty lips. Her face is soft ivory, her hands are fine with delicate veins, her eyes are Irish blue, her brows are dark, her hair is dark brown, wavy, she blushes faint roses. She has on a little straw hat with blue ribbon the color of a robin's egg, a bow like a butterfly at the side...

I go outside and see Mr. McDowell and Randy counting the eight cases — four Honee Orange and four ginger ale that Mr. McDowell has just bought.

Mr. McDowell gives Randy the money.

Nine dollars and sixty cents.

"Okay," says Randy. "Go back down the cellar there, Martin — we gotta do somethin' about that name, right, Mr. McDowell? — and catch these cases while Mr. McDowell and I make sure he gets what he's paid for!"

Then Randy, behind Mr. McDowell's back, winks at me when our eyes meet, and the wink gives me a chill.

Mr. McDowell just paid for six cases of his own drinks from his own cellar. We're thieves. I'm a thief!

When I'm finished in the cellar and close the trap door I go over to where she is standing near some shelves and whisper to her, "What's your name?"

"Gerty," she says and looks down at the silver buckles on her shoes. "Gerty McDowell."

Her electric blue blouse has a V-opening down to where her division is. She has a hankie in the pocket, fluffed up. There's perfume all around.

I swallow so hard that I think my Adam's apple is going to come up into my mouth. I see my eyes in hers. Is that possible?

Can a person say a million things in the blink of an eye and not say one word? Is it magic to talk just with your eyes? Can everybody do that? Can everybody understand eye talk?

Like I can?

I go out and get in the truck.

Randy's got my wallet. He's zipping it back up.

"I've decided to give you a nickname, Martin. And it's a good one. You're going to like it. It's perfect for you. Boy. Boy O'Boy! Get it? Boy, oh boy! Isn't that great? Isn't that funny? Get it?"

I can't say anything.

Randy again.

"And, oh yeah, I see by yer birth certificate yer not sixteen years of age. You lied to Mr. Mirsky. He'll fire you if he finds out, you know.

"Boy, it doesn't matter how big the lie is or how small the lie is. You are a liar. Simple as that. A liar is a liar. And your lovely, kind Jew Mirsky wouldn't be too happy with you, would he, if he found out you were a liar, now, would he?

"And another thing. You get fired for lying, everybody will know. This is Ottawa and the Ottawa Valley. Everybody knows about everybody up and down the rivers of the Ottawa Valley."

It's quiet this morning on Sweetland Avenue except for the roar of truck number 15.

Fifteen. My age.

"You know, Boy," says Randy. "The sign of a good helper is not if he's strong or a good worker or fast or anything like that. No, no. The sign of a good helper is if he does what he's told and keeps his mouth shut about it."

I'm staring straight ahead.

Randy's looking at me, not the road.

We're not moving very fast. Ahead at a stop light is an empty flatbed truck. The back edge of it is like a knife. Randy's still looking over at me.

"...what he's told and keeps his mouth shut about it..."

My legs are jammed into the floor. My hands shoot out onto the dashboard.

"Stop!" I'm screaming. "Watch out! STOP!"

Randy glides to an easy stop nowhere near the truck ahead.

Everything is quiet except my breathing.

"What's the matter with you, Boy? Are you crazy?"

4

Spy

EVERY DAY after work I go to the punch clock. Above the clock there is a big board with enough slots in it to hold a card for each person who works at Pure Spring. I lift my card from my slot and dip it into the clock. The clock chungs and a bell rings. I pull out my card and read it. It gives the date and the time. I've worked an hour overtime today. That's probably why I'm so tired. I reach up and drop the card back into its slot. Sore arms.

There's a note sticking up. It's from Anita. She wants me to go to her office.

Anita's at her desk. Frilly blue blouse this time. Lots of lipstick and perfume. Eyelashes waving like fans.

"Right choo are!" she says and shows me with her hand the chair across from her. Her arm jingles with many colored bracelets.

"How's it going with Randy?"

"Okay, I guess."

"Okay?"

"Yeah. It's okay. Everything's okay."

"Well, that's good to hear. Sometimes Randy is...Well, you see, Mr. Mirsky is always doing things, favors for people, and he hired Randy because he's the son of an old friend of Mr. Mirsky's. You see, when Randy was around fifteen or so, he fell out of the Ferris wheel at the Ottawa Exhibition — fell right on his head — and he's never been quite right since."

"He is kind of strange," I say softly.

"He's had it rough. As if falling out of a Ferris wheel on your noggin wasn't bad enough, his mother a little later ran off with some crazy Communist to start a colony somewhere where nobody would own anything but at the same time everybody would own everything.

"And on top of that, just last year, last December, Randy's younger brother was killed in an accident while the Canadian soldiers were arriving in Pusan, Korea, getting ready to fight the Commies there."

Buz, I'm thinking. Buz.

"Anyway, Randy's starting to fall apart, in my opinion. I'd fire him in a minute but Mr. Mirsky won't. Always wants to give him a chance. There's been complaints about him recently. Maybe stealing from the customers."

"Stealing?" I say.

"Yeah. And some rumors are going around about Randy and his weird ideas."

"Weird ideas?"

"Yeah. Weird ideas. Anyway, he seems interested in you. Asked to see your application form the other day."

"He asked to see my form?"

"Yeah. Not a bad thing, I guess. Get to know who you're working with. By the way, your grampa, Rip Sawyer. I've met him. He used to work with old man Mirsky, using pure spring water filtering out of the limestone, Nanny Goat Hill, you know, Bronson and Wellington, Booth and Wellington streets — around there. Good man, Rip Sawyer. Honest as the day is long, as they say."

"I'm really hungry. I think I better get home for supper," I say, trying not to be rude.

"Oh, I'm sorry, Martin. How thoughtless of me. Of course you're hungry. It's past seven o'clock. A little overtime money, eh? Well, I'd better get to the point, eh? Right choo are. Here's what I'd like you to do. Could you kind of keep an eye on Randy? See if you can spot any funny business going on with Randy and our customers? Just between you and me?"

On the streetcar going home, my stomach is growling, my arms are aching from lifting cases.

And I'm thinking over and over again.

How am I supposed to spy on a guy who's blackmailing me?

5

Sap's Running

A T HOME on the radio Nat "King" Cole is still singing the song "Too Young."

All day today in the stores and restaurants where we stopped you could hear radios playing the song "Too Young" by Nat "King" Cole. I love the sound of his voice. Deep, strong, soft, kind of raspy.

I love the way he says the word "love." He pronounces it "lawv" — "They try to tell us we're too young...to really be in lawv."

I could listen to this song forever. The violins. The piano.

Grampa Rip is saying stuff about getting some maple syrup.

"The sap's running," he's saying. "Just oozing out of the trees, filling up the pails. Perfect weather for it. Warm in the day, cool in the night. That's what you need..."

Grampa Rip's mind is jumping all around. It's not a

good thing. Usually it means that soon his mind will go away for a while.

"And don't forget, when you brush yer hair, pull the hairs out of the brush and take them and shove them into the corners of the screens so's the birds can pick at them for to make their nests…and we're goin' to plant some catnip seeds in pots for Cheap, put them in the windows, lots of water and sunshine…grow in no time…"

Grampa and I are eating our supper.

Grampa loves potatoes. Tonight there's fried potatoes and there'll be enough left over for breakfast. He also loves pork. Roast pork. Pork hocks. Fried pork, pork pie, pork steak, stuffed pork, boiled pork, pork stew, pork and beans, cabbage and pork…

Tonight it's fried pork.

I'm chewing and listening to Grampa Rip with one ear and with my other ear I'm listening to Randy in the truck today.

Today in the truck Randy started asking me questions.

"Are you a Communist?"

"A what?"

"A Communist. A Red."

"I don't know."

"You don't know what a Commie is?"

"No."

"A Commie is a guy who believes everything should be shared by everybody with everybody. Like for instance if I had ten dollars and you had zero dollars I should give you five of my dollars so's we'd be even."

"Share everything?"

"Everything."

One of our customers today was the Russian Embassy on Charlotte Street right around the corner from Baron Strathcona's fountain at the top of Strathcona Park. We stopped in front of a big locked iron gate.

A small iron gate in the middle of the big gate opened and we went in. Randy told me I was to go in with the guard and he'd show me where the cases were kept. He told me to bring out five cases of empty quarts and then bring in five cases of full quarts, all ginger ale.

"They love ginger ale," he said. "They must guzzle it down with their vodka." Then he said, "And don't make any mistakes! We don't cheat these guys. If they thought we were cheating them they'd probably shoot us on the spot, no questions asked!"

I had to carry five cases down a set of iron stairs to a metal room one at a time and then one at a time carry five empties up. Ten trips!

The guard who watched me the whole time looked strong enough to lift Randy's whole load of two hundred cases all at once. His shoulders were like basketballs and his head was like a pumpkin. He could have picked skinny little Randy up and used him as a toothpick. I thought that if this guard worked at McDowell's Grocery and Lunch on Sweetland instead of that rickety old man, Randy never would have cheated him out of one cent! The little coward.

Also, I thought if this guard here is a Communist, why

isn't he sharing these trips with me? Five trips each? Commies are supposed to share everything equally, aren't they?

During one trip we looked at each other. He looked right in my eyes. I looked right in his. I tried to see Russia in there but I couldn't. Share and share alike? No sign of it.

I went out and sat in the truck. Through the small iron gate in the big one I could see Randy being paid and a tall man in a gray suit signing the bill.

I tell Grampa a little bit about the Russian Embassy but he's only half listening. He wants to talk about his visit today at McEvoy's Funeral Home on Kent Street.

"You know, Martin," he says, "today at McEvoy's I met a man I haven't seen in over sixty years! Imagine! Sixty years! And, Martin, I have to tell ya, I made a joke that made a bunch of them at the funeral laugh out loud. He said, 'Rip, is that you?' and I said, 'Yes it is, Dermit.' And then I said this. I said, 'As I was saying before we were so rudely interrupted by the passage of sixty years, how's everything going, anyway?' Ya see, Martin, I pretended that we were resuming a conversation that had only been interrupted for a moment, not sixty odd years ago."

Grampa's going into one of his slippages. That's what he calls them. I'll keep an eye on him. That's one of my jobs.

We wash up the supper dishes and I decide to see if Grampa wants to take a stroll, get him some fresh air, calm him down a bit.

Down on the corner of Bank Street and Somerset in front of Borden's Dairy a boy and a girl are licking their ice cream cones and then kissing each other.

"Go ahead," Grampa says, soft to himself. "Spring in Ottawa is very short indeed, as is life itself."

We pass some very old men in front of the Ritz Hotel standing around smoking pipes and talking about spring.

"You know, Martin, I once knew an old fella with a perforated eardrum. He had a really funny trick he could do. He'd take a big suck on his pipe and blow the smoke out of the side of his head!"

After a stroll down to the Rialto theater where you can see three movies, a serial, a short, a cartoon and a newsreel for fifteen cents and where Grampa Rip, who knows everybody, knows Kelly O'Kelly, the world's oldest movie usher, we're back to the corner of Somerset and Bank.

The Somerset streetcar is stalled there because the trolley has slipped off the electric wire. The pole of the trolley is rubbing on the wire and there are silver and gold sparks showering down. The streetcar conductor gets out and shuts the streetcar doors so people won't sneak on when he's not looking.

There's a little crowd stopping to watch. The conductor is a huge handsome man with lots of beautiful wavy gray hair showing under his cap. His shoulders are as wide as a doorway.

Grampa Rip knows him, of course.

"That's Pete Lowell," Grampa Rip tells me. "Once,

when Pete was young, when he first started with the old Ottawa Electric Railway, a streetcar he was driving slipped off the track right on this very corner. It was Christmas and the car was packed with people — Christmas shoppers loaded down with parcels. Pete got out and examined the situation. Then he got back in the streetcar and made a little speech. He told them that what he usually did in these situations was he'd ask the people to kindly get off the streetcar for a moment while he lifted it back onto the track but since it was Christmas and they had so many parcels he didn't want to inconvenience them so it would be all right if they just stayed right where they were and hang on and be quiet and don't move around and he'd be right back.

"Then he went out and lifted the streetcar — people, parcels and all — back onto the track. Strongest man in Ottawa back in those days. Famous for it."

Pete Lowell is now pulling down on the trolley rope, swinging the trolley pole back and forward until the wheel is ready to touch the electric wire and the sparks are firing across the blue-black spring sky and the small crowd gives up a cheer when the wheel hits the wire and the lights of the streetcar glow back on and the motor goes back humming and the people inside start talking to each other about what just happened.

"Good evening, Rip Sawyer. Haven't seen you in a while," says Conductor Pete Lowell. He's heading back to get back into his streetcar, lots of the passengers watching as he walks.

"It's a grand evening, Pete Lowell," says Grampa Rip.

And some of the people watching have looks on their faces that make you think that they wish big Pete Lowell, famous streetcar conductor, would say good evening to them, too. They'd be glad if he did. Maybe even proud.

It's time to take Grampa Rip home to bed. He needs a rest. So do I. Tired. Worked hard today. Carrying, lifting, bending. Stealing.

Here's a little spring rain coming. Sweet.

Soon there are puddles like tiny silver mirrors on the Somerset Street sidewalk.

We head back home by way of Cooper Street, past the Producers Dairy horse stables.

Grampa Rip likes to cut through the stables and into the Borden's Dairy stables, which are even bigger, to get back to Somerset Street and our place.

The Borden's stables has two stories. There could be more than fifty horses in here.

All to deliver the milk every day except Sunday.

"But the trucks will soon take over," Grampa Rip is saying. "The horse-drawn wagon is about to be no more. A new time is beginning, Martin. Your time."

There's the smell of the horse hay and horse balls and horse breath and horse piss and horse meat and horse spit and harness and fermenting oats.

"Worker horses," says Grampa Rip. "Horses that work for a living — those are the horses I like. They're like men workers who work and women workers who work..."

And the horses are shaking their big handsome heads, rattling harness hanging there and snorting and blowing sometimes out their noses making the flapping sound.

"...it's not how big you are or how pretty you are or how strong you are or how fast you are..."

And the beautiful shivering horse-body flesh and the thumps from the horse stalls stomping now and then and horses laughing deep from their throats, horse throats and chuckling deep and grunting glad to be home.

"...it's how reliable you are and how honest you are," says Grampa Rip.

At home Cheap is on Grampa's giant rocking chair. He lies there like he's dead — on his back, his paws sticking up. But he's just pretending, acting. He does this just to make me worried.

"You're not dead, too," I say to Cheap. "You're just pretending..."

He rolls over and starts licking his toes, making Grampa Rip's rocker rock. Grampa told me once they like to have their toes clean so's they can have — in case anything quick and dangerous happens — a clean getaway.

I can hear the oil furnace go on. The night is cold. Good for the maple syrup. Humming goes the furnace.

I feed Cheap.

"Now?" says Cheap. "Now?"

I bring Grampa Rip his cocoa and his Bible and his beads. He's in his long pajama gown and he's got his night-cap on with the little tassel hanging. He's sitting up in bed. He has his hands clasped over his potbelly with his prayer beads woven through his big fingers. He looks calm and pleased.

"I'm going to a funeral wake tomorrow," he says.

"That's nice," I say. He goes to one nearly every day.

"Yes," he says. "I like funeral wakes."

"I know you do, Grampa Rip."

"Yes, funeral wakes are good to go to. You can meet a lot of wonderful people from the past at a funeral wake. Oddly enough, my boy, one of the grandest places to meet the living is where they all come to honor their dead." He takes a sip of his cocoa and opens his Bible anywhere.

"God bless you," he says to me, looking in my eyes. "God bless you, whoever you are." He doesn't remember who I am.

"Goodnight, Grampa," I say.

Cheap gets back in the giant rocker to wash his face. The rocker moves. Sometimes when that happens, Grampa Rip Sawyer thinks that it's *his* grampa, Hack Sawyer, in the chair, come back to haunt us.

Grampa Rip sleeps with his open hand on top of his head. Fingers spread out over his bald head and his nightcap which is half off — like somebody who just remembered something very important and has just slapped himself over the head saying, "Oh my God, I just remembered I didn't turn off the stove. The fried potatoes will be burnt black!"

I go to the front window to pull down the blind. In the foggy windowpane I see the face of Gerty McDowell. The butterfly on her straw hat.

I wipe the window and Gerty disappears.

Under the streetlight, across the street, sitting on the park bench in the light rain with his gray coat.

It's the Gray Man, again.

It's also the man I saw today signing the Pure Spring bill at the Russian Embassy!

What Happened • Two

Y OU WERE *walking with your father across Angel Square. Then down York Street and to the corner of Friel Street where Horrors Leblanc lived.*

Your father was talking most of the way about how Phil was getting worse. The older Phil got the harder he was to handle. He'll never be right, you have to face that.

You always knew that. You wondered was your father only just finding that out now? Hadn't you known that ever since you could remember?

"Since the baby died your mother's never been the same," your father said. "It's getting harder and harder to take care of Phil. He's a handful and more."

Then he changed the subject. He didn't want to talk about this any more.

Your mother always told you that Phil was born at five to midnight at the end of the day, and you came into this world ten minutes later at five after midnight at the beginning of the day.

The end. The beginning. Poor Phil.

Your father worked in the same office as his friend Horrors Leblanc.

"Horrors was always a good sport," your father started, changing the subject. "Once we took a fish, a catfish, and nailed it with a half a dozen roofing nails, the short nails with the big heads, to the underside of Horrors Leblanc's wooden chair that he sat in every day at his desk.

"Soon the fish began to rot and stink and everybody in the big office who came up to Horrors' desk would wonder why it was that Horrors smelled so bad.

"Horrors searched everywhere — all through his desk, emptied out all the drawers, and even took up the rug and looked — but couldn't find out where the horrible smell was coming from. He never thought to turn his chair upside down and look there...and for days and days everybody in the office was saying, 'Why is it that Horrors smells so horrible?'"

He wanted you to see the humor. But you wouldn't.

"Was it funny?" you said.

"Yes, it was FUNNY!" he said. "Anyway, Horrors is lending us his car because of this very important trip we have to take."

You were silent.

"Very important trip," he repeated.

You were still silent. You knew that if you asked what it was, he wouldn't tell you. You looked at the scar on his forehead right between the eyes.

"Most important trip this family will ever take."

"What trip? Where are we going?" you asked.

"You'll see," he said.

6

Wedding Pictures

I'M IN the truck waiting for Randy.

Grampa was okay this morning. Because he slept so nice. Sometimes when the slippage is on he doesn't sleep so calm. Sleeps like a freight train. Last night he didn't know who I was. But he knew me this morning very well. That was good.

"Revelly! Revelly!" he shouted me awake. Imitating a bugle. "Revelly! Up, Martin! Up, my lad!

> "Clay lies still but blood's a rover;
> Breath's a ware that will not keep.
> Up lad; when the journey's over
> There'll be time enough for sleep."

He has called out this poem many times to get me up. I know it off by heart. Grampa Rip loves poems.

Back to me in the truck.

We're moving now and Randy's silent for quite a while.

Then, "Know what a coincidence is, Boy? A coincidence? It's two things that happen together and turn out to be a big surprise."

Here we go.

"Looked at yer job application. Seen yer address. Somerset Street. Number 511, Apartment 4. Right across from Dumb Donald Park. Here's what you call a coincidence! I used to live there! Right across the hall. Apartment three. Right across the hall from four! Can you imagine?

"I lived there before I got married. Before I worked for Pure Spring.

"And do you know who lived right where yer livin now, with yer grandfather what's his name — a funny name, Mr. Rip is it? You know who lived there? Can you guess? Guess. Guess who lived there!"

How am I supposed to guess this? What does he want?

"Esther Williams?" I say.

"Ya can't guess? I'll give you a hint. It's something to do with where we were yesterday."

Yesterday! Gerty. Gerty McDowell. McDowell's Grocery and Lunch on Sweetland. Sweet Gerty.

Gerty lived where I live now?

"Was it Gerty McDowell?"

"Gerty McDowell! Who the hell is Gerty McDowell? What kind of a guess is that? No! Yesterday. The Russian Embassy!"

I'm thinking was it pumpkin head, the guard?

"No guess, pretty boy? Well I'll tell ya! It was *Igor*. Igor, the famous Russian spy guy. Igor Gouzenko! Yeah! He lived right where yer livin' now! Blew the whistle on a bunch of Commies in Ottawa! Big scandal. The RCMP came. The Russians came. They wanted to kill him because he ratted on them. He worked at the Russian Embassy. He was a cipher clerk. Figured out code messages. Secret stuff. And he *lived* right where yer livin' now! He's famous. And ya never heard of him! Kids these days! Don't know anything. It's all they can do, some of them, like my last helper, to get to work before 7:00 A.M. in the morning!"

I think I do remember something I heard on the radio about Igor. Igor the Russian who changed sides. He wasn't exactly a spy. But I don't want to argue.

"You don't say 7:00 A.M. in the morning. A.M. *is* the morning. A is for ante. M is for meridiem which means *noon*. It's Latin. You say 7:00 in the morning or you say 7:00 A.M. You don't say both. It's *redundant* to say both."

"Latin. Smarty boy, eh, Boy! Yer not one of *those*, are ya, pretty boy? A smarty pants sissy, you know what I'm sayin'? A homo, a faggy, a fruity fruit, an airy fairy, a little pansy wansy nancy, a queer duck?…"

Randy smells like Aqua Velva shaving lotion and BO. His fingernails are dirty. His ears are scaly. His skin is rough. His teeth are brown and crooked. His voice is high and hoarse. He's skinny and he always looks like he could use a bath. His hair is full of Wildroot Cream-Oil grease. His hair is big and there's a fat coil of it hanging down the middle of his forehead that bounces up and down when he's excited. Like now.

Randy's always telling me about himself. What a great dancer he is. What a great lover he is…

"Anyway, he escaped, Igor did, and to this day — that was six years ago, nobody knows where he went. And the Ruskies, they're still lookin' for him. Fer a long time they had agents conducting surveying at the apartment building, sittin' in the park across the street all day…"

He means surveillance, not surveying.

"Those were the days when I lived there. Right across the hall from where you live now! Single guy like me. All the women I wanted.

"Those were the days. Boy! Every job I had there'd be women around who wanted Randy. I did roofing for a while. Doing a roof one time in Rockcliffe Village where all the rich people live, a woman took me right off the roof right into her bedroom window. Randy the roofer! Right into the rich woman's bed! How 'bout that?

"And I delivered bread fer a time. When the sign in the window said NO BREAD TODAY, that was the sign that her husband was away…Randy the breadman…And for a while I was a driving instructor teaching people, women, how to drive a car. They'd be so scared driving around the Experimental Farm I'd take them into the backseat and calm them down. 'Oh, Randy!' they'd say. 'When do I get my next lesson?' And another time I was a door-to-door vacuum-cleaner salesman. Boy, you wouldn't believe it. 'Come on in, Randy, and demonstrate yer vacuum!' Right there on the living-room rug if you know what I mean. Those were the days…"

While Randy is babbling away about himself I'm thinking about Gerty, her eyes. Did I see my own eyes in hers? How is that possible, how can that be? Does that mean I love myself?

My window is open. There's a warm spring breeze. I've got the shirt-sleeves of my Pure Spring shirt rolled up. With my elbow out the window like this, my biceps muscle shows the rolled-up sleeve tight around it.

Grampa Rip showed me how to build up my biceps. With two cans of Habitant pea soup. Large size. One for each hand. You lift the cans from your waist up to your chin — left, right, left, right — one hundred times each.

I wonder if Gerty will notice my muscles. Habitant soup muscles.

We pull into the yard of Persephone's Grocery, a big store on Beechwood Avenue.

Randy gives me my instructions. Many instructions. Instructions to steal.

Looks like I'm doing *all* the work this time. *All* the stealing.

"What are you going to do while I'm carrying all of these cases?" I say.

Randy looks at me. Squints his eyes. Looks at me hard.

"See the guy standing, waiting at that big shed there? He's in charge of what goes in and what comes out of that shed. He's gonna want cream soda, Honee Orange, Grapefruit 'N Lime, Minted Grape and, of course, ginger ale. First I'll go in with him and check it out. Then we'll come out. He'll have it written down. He'll tell you how many. Here's what you do. You'll put *one* less full case than he says. *One* full case less of *each* color. Got it?"

"I don't want to do this..."

He squints hard at me again.

"Mr. Mirsky's going to be very, very disappointed in you, pretty boy, when I have a little chat with him. Show him your birth certificate."

I tear the wallet out of my pocket, unzip it.

No birth certificate. He has stolen my birth certificate!

"Don't worry," says Randy, real friendly. "It's safe with me for now. You'll get it back later. I promise. Now, let's go! Partner."

"He's going to see me..."

"He won't be lookin' at you..."

"Why not? That's his job, isn't it?"

"He won't be doin' his job."

"What do you mean?"

"He'll be looking at these..." Randy takes a handful of photographs out of his shirt pocket. "I'm going to show him my wedding pictures..." says Randy.

He wants three cases of cream soda, three of Grapefruit 'N Lime. On the dolly, I deliver two of each into the shed, pile them on some already full cases. He wants four Minted Grape, he gets three. Six Honee Orange, he gets five. He wants ten cases of ginger ale, he gets nine. The ten cases are piled up on top of the other colors, burying them. You can't tell how much has been delivered.

The whole time Randy and the guy in charge of shipping have their backs to me whooping and ho-ho-ing and giggling. Not seeing me at all, not watching.

Time to take out the empties. Now Randy's helping. Even the shipping guy is helping. And we're all counting — counting twice, double-checking, seeing everything is accurate. Twenty-six cases exactly…oh, Randy, you are so honest…the *exact* amount of empties.

The shipper pays Randy for twenty-six cases of drinks. He doesn't know it but he only got twenty-one.

Time to go. The shipper shakes hands with Randy and even slaps him on the back! Good old Randy. See you next time!

We're on St. Patrick Street heading west. Randy's telling me all about how he is like a fisherman's lure to women. He is bait! A juicy worm. And when they'd bite, he'd hook them and pull them in, right in the boat, all the women…

"You see, I've got the charm, the wavy hair, the teeth, the muscles, the aftershave. I'm a great dancer. I've got the know-how. They can't resist. I'm bait…"

I'm looking at the pictures…wedding pictures?

Naked men and women. Dozens of photographs of real people doing everything you could think of to each other — lying down, standing up, upside down, up on ladders, two men and a woman, two women and a man, two men and two women. Sticking, licking, dripping. A woman with a donkey, a man with a sheep…

I look up. An empty logging truck is slowing down in front of us. I'm yelling, "Watch out! STOP!"

Randy's pushing me. "What's wrong with you! Don't

you think I know how to drive! What's wrong with you! Smarten up! Straighten up! What 'r' ya afraid of...I'm going to run into somebody?..."

He's yelling stuff at me. I feel sick. I lean out my window and throw up on to the pavement. Randy pulls over. I get out. I'm hanging on to a foot rail on a telephone pole. I'm retching. The wedding pictures are all over the sidewalk.

"Hey, you puked all over my pictures!"

Randy is trying to help me stand up.

When I was small, my friend Billy Batson and I used to climb up telephone poles like this one. But Billy's gone now from Papineau Street where we used to live and it's a secret where he went because his mother wants to live where his crazy father will never find them.

Up and up those foot rails we'd climb so high, Billy and me, almost to the wires on top and look out, pretending we were on the mast of a tall ship at sea, and we'd shout, "Ship ahoy! Ship ahoy! Pirate ship ahoy!..."

Like we were heroes in a pirate movie and nothing, nothing could ever hurt us.

7

Exploding Trees

CHEAP'S FUR is ruffling and his eyes are half closed and his only ear is flapping in the wind. He's in the basket of my bicycle. We're heading to Sweetland Avenue on this Sunday in the spring. Watch out we don't get the front wheel of the bicycle caught in the streetcar track, eh, Cheap!

We're on Laurier Avenue heading toward the Sweetland Grocery and Lunch and Gerty McDowell.

The bells of St. Joseph's Church are dinging and donging. You can see the bells up there swinging. And the clapper in each bell waiting to hit each pretty curved side.

Grampa Rip planted some catnip seeds this morning in a pot and we put it in the windowsill.

"The sun and this water will do the work," says Grampa Rip.

There are girls skipping rope on the sandy sidewalk. There are melting lumps of snow disappearing down the laneways. And little rivers running.

Another robin!

Spring is trying to come.

The trees want to explode.

And the flowers want to drive their heads up through the soft earth in all the parks.

This afternoon, right after lunch, Grampa Rip left the apartment all dressed up in his watch and chain to go to McEvoy's and another funeral wake. I'll be home at five to meet him and we'll make the supper together.

I'm wearing my Pure Spring shirt because it looks so good on me. I washed it last night and this morning Grampa helped me iron it without burning a big hole in the back of it.

I have the sleeves rolled up to show my biceps. A hundred times each with the cans of Habitant soup at noon today makes the biceps swell and push tight against the roll of the sleeves.

Will she remember me?

Last night I dreamt a dream that Cheap was in love with a cat with silk stockings and pale-blue panties with rose-pink-colored ribbon trim and big blue eyes and wavy brown hair and a little straw hat with a bow and pouty lips just like Gerty's.

Will she ever find out that I stole from her store? Will it show on my face?

I park my bike, put Cheap in his harness and leash and then my heart sinks from my chest down to the sidewalk.

The store is closed! Of course it's closed. It's Sunday! But wait. The lunch part is open. It's a different door.

Cheap stays beside me while I open the door. We go in. Together. We're partners.

There are three booths and four stools. The smell is fried onions and vanilla milkshakes.

There are two customers. Lovers, it looks like. They're in the end booth farthest from the door. The milkshake machine is buzzing away. They're getting a plate with two hamburgers on it. They're not sitting across from each other in the booth. They're both on one side. Sitting close. Hamburgers on one plate, not two.

Their waiter is Gerty. Gerty herself. She has on a long white apron tied at the back. No straw hat. A ribbon this time tying her hair over one shoulder. Blue.

I sit on the first of the four stools and put Cheap on the second stool and stroke him hard so he'll stay.

She comes around the counter, pours the milkshake out of the metal container into a tall glass jar and punches in two straws and takes the milkshake over to the lovers. She comes back behind the counter.

I have big plans for what I'm going to say. Tell her I stole. Tell her she's beautiful and I love her. Tell her I dreamt that my cat was in love with a female cat that looked just like her...

But here's what I say: "Set up a vanilla shake fer me, heavy on the vanilla and a double saucer of straight cream for my partner here, the thicker the better!"

I've seen a thousand cowboy movies. I'm one of those cowboys ordering drinks in the saloon.

Cheap looks up at me. He's never heard my voice like

this. He thinks for a second I'm somebody else. His ear goes back.

She turns and with her back to us pours the ice cream and milk and vanilla and puts it in the mixer. She pours a saucer of cream. She puts both in front of us. Her eyes are sparkling. She's got a little smile. She got the cowboy joke right away.

"I was wondering if I'd see you again," she says, and I nearly fall off the stool.

Soon a pretty lady comes in — a lady shaped like a pear, and comes behind the counter and takes Gerty's apron and puts it on.

"Thank you, dear," she says.

Gerty comes and sits on the other side of Cheap. Cheap is standing on the stool with his front paws on the counter licking up his cream that was ordered for him by some stranger from an old cowboy movie.

"Do you take your cat with you everywhere you go?"

"Sometimes."

"What's his name? Is it a him?"

"His name's Cheap."

"Cheep. Like a bird noise?"

"No. Cheap. He cost ten cents."

She thinks I'm funny! She laughs a happy laugh and throws her brown hair over her other shoulder.

"My grampa has a cat," she says. "It just sleeps and eats and, well, you know. It's got no personality and probably a very tiny brain…"

"Was that your grampa in the store last week?"

"Yes. He's not feeling very well. He's weak. He's trying to sell the store."

"Is he too weak to go down the cellar?"

She nods. She wrinkles her brow, making a sad face.

I knew it. That's why it was so easy for Randy to steal from him. Randy and I. Stealing from the weak.

"When you first came in I thought you were working but it's Sunday so I wondered. Isn't that your work shirt...Pure Spring shirt..."

She's peering at the shoulder. Close to me. She smells like...what...lilacs?

"Do you work here and in the store?" I ask, stuck for something — anything — to say.

"No," she says. "Just filling in when the regular waitress is on her break."

We go out. I put Cheap in the basket and we walk my bike down to Strathcona Park.

The water's not turned on yet in Baron Strathcona's fountain. But it will be soon.

She tells me all about herself. Her father — she doesn't remember him — was killed in the war. In his pictures he's very handsome. She'll show me sometime. Her mother died last spring. Tuberculosis. TB. She was tired all the time. Then coughing up blood. Gerty quit school to stay home and take care of her mother. She didn't go back. Now she lives in the house next door to the store with her grampa...

"I live with a grampa, too..." I say.

A grampa. It sounds so stupid.

We're silent walking along. She's waiting, I know, for

me to tell her everything about me. Fair is fair. But I don't.
I can't.

Strathcona Park is almost covered in ice water. The
snow is melting so fast that you can hear the water gur-
gling everywhere. They've already dynamited the ice on
the Rideau River and the water is deep and fast. The river
is full, bursting.

Sounds of water slurping, burbling everywhere.

And redwing blackbirds are back — *Konk-a-ree! Konk-
a-ree!* — up and down the riverbank and in our ears.
Cheap is glaring at the birds.

Gerty gets a little unfriendly because I didn't share.

"Why do you wear that shirt even when you're not
working? Don't you have a shirt of your own?"

"Grampa Rip told me it looked good on me and so I
put it on to come and see you."

"For me?" She's friendly again.

"Yes."

"It does look very good on you. With sleeves rolled and
everything and so nicely ironed! Who ironed it?"

"I ironed it. Grampa Rip showed me. I can sew, too.
And cook. I can cook. Grampa Rip says that a man who
can't iron and wash and sew and cook is not a man as far
as he's concerned!"

Gerty likes what I just said. I can see in her face the way
she looks at me.

Thank you, Grampa Rip.

On our way back, Gerty walks beside me this time
instead of on the other side of the bicycle.

In front of her house her little finger touches my little finger.

"When does the Pure Spring truck come back again?" she says.

"Not for another week or so, according to my boss, Randy," I say.

"That's too bad," says Gerty, and then with a small smile she blushes because of what she just said.

Cheap and I whiz like bullets home. We're late.

The maple tree is about to explode above the Gray Man on the bench in Dundonald Park across the street from our apartment on Somerset Street where the famous spy smasher, Igor, once lived.

I forgot to turn off the radio when I left today. Grampa won't like that. Wastes electricity, he says.

While I'm opening the door, Nat "King" Cole is just finishing up his beautiful song — "...we're not too young to know / This love will last..."

Now the violins and piano finish it off...

But no Grampa Rip.

He's late. He's never late.

Something's wrong.

Now there's noise outside. I open the door.

It's Grampa Rip. He's with a very short sandy-colored man in an army uniform that's too big for him. His nose is very red and his eyes are close together. His army boots seem way too big for him. He clicks his heels together and snaps to attention and salutes me. He's looking up at me, staring with his tiny eyes. Green eyes. The fingers of his saluting hand are stubby and red and the nails are bitten down short. He holds his salute.

There's a bowl of pennies and nickels and dimes on the hall table. Grampa always puts his change in there.

"His name is Sandy," says Grampa Rip. "He found me. I got lost. He brought me home. I'm tired. Give him fifty cents out of the bowl."

Grampa pats Sandy on his sandy-colored head. Grampa's big hand covers the head.

"He's a friend of mine. We go away back. I'm goin' to bed."

I give Sandy five dimes and he salutes again.

Then, down the stairs, his big boots bang-banging and he's gone.

8

Honee Orange and Tulips

"**I**'M VERY matutinal this morning," Grampa is saying after reveille and an extra verse of "Up Lad" (there'll be time enough for sleep after you're dead). He's been up since 5:00 A.M. in the morning. Said he was starving after a wonderful night's sleep. Frying up a batch of pork rinds.

"Matutinal?" I say.

"Right!" he says. "Latin for the Greek goddess of dawn, Matuta! Very handy word. Impress your friends with knowledge. Be the most popular kid on the block!"

I get to the Pure Spring truck early. I look in the window and see my birth certificate on the seat. He's giving it back to me. I slip it in my wallet.

"You're early," Randy says behind me.

"I'm very *matutinal* this morning," I say.

"Yeah, right, smart ass! I figure I'd give your birth certificate back. I felt sorry for ya. You were sick and crazy there. I got worried. Maybe I was a bit hard on ya. Maybe we can be pals? No hard feelings?" He puts out his hand. "Shake?"

I take my hand out of my pocket and put it out. His hand is small and hard and rough and strong. We shake.

"Pals?" says Randy.

"Mm," I say.

I don't think I ever said "mm" in my whole life before. It sounds like yes but not quite.

Maybe Randy's not so bad after all. A liar and a thief, yes. But, so am I. So am I a liar and a thief.

We drive off. Lots of silence.

Then Randy: "What's this fancy word business? Why cancha talk English? Ya said you were *what* this morning?"

"Matutinal," I say.

"Ma toot in al…"

"Greek goddess of dawn — Matuta. Means you like the morning. A morning person. I was up early because my Grampa Rip couldn't sleep because he was hungry —"

"Matoota! Well, why don't you just say you got up early? Why do you wanna say all this nutty stuff? I thought we were pals…my last helper was useless, he was lazy and stoopid and he picked his nose and ate it but at least he didn't come up with all this baloney about Latin words and Greek goddesses and crap. What's wrong with you anyway?"

Inside, I'm smiling. Two reasons. One. I'm making a list of everything we've ever stolen — the name of the store, the date, the number of cases, the method. Two, I'm smiling because of Gerty. Because of you, Gerty! Now I'm not so afraid of Randy any more. I've got much nicer things to think about.

Randy is back on the subject of how charming he is.

"I like 'em tall, I like 'em short, I like 'em skinny, I like 'em chubby. It don't matter...they all come to Randy... they can't help themselves..."

I'm drinking my one free Honee Orange for the day and eating peanuts. Randy lifted two bags on our way out of our last store without paying for them.

Do stolen peanuts taste better than bought peanuts? Randy says they do. And, oh, they taste so warm, Gerty, it's like chewing sweet bark and the salt on them on your tongue and the crunchiness and the butternutty sunflowery orange smell of the oil on them and when you stick your nose right into the package you get all of it specially when you lick the salt, stick your tongue inside and lick the cellophane...and pour down the warm Honee Orange, down your throat until it feels smooth and sweet and it makes your nose squeeze up it's so delicious, and then you're not thirsty any more for a while and...what's Randy talking about now...?

"...tulips. Boy oh boy I can hardly wait for all those tulips to come up. You know what a tulip reminds me of?"

"What," I say.

"Guess," says Randy.

I can guess but I won't.

"I don't know," I say.

"A woman's patootie, banana brain!"

Banana brain? Where does he get these brilliant sayings? Patootie?

"Anyway, the tulips in Ottawa when they come up they all come from Holland, did ya know that? I was over in Holland in the war. The women, the girls really loved old Randy over there, you know what I'm sayin'? Their favorite Canuck was yours truly and you better believe it. Near wore me out, they did! Come closer to killin' me than the Germans did and that's the truth!"

What was that last thing she said to me? Could you come to me sooner? No, it wasn't that. When will I see you again? No. She said when does the truck come again. I said a week or so. She said, "That's too bad." What beautiful words. That's. Too. Bad. Like music.

Randy again: "But no more of that for Randy. Cause ol' Randy's married now. Settled down. Got the most beautiful...you ever see the movie *Neptune's Daughter* starring Esther Williams? Technicolor? Esther sells bathing suits. Designs them or something. Every five minutes she comes out in a new bathing suit. Drives ya crazy! This handsome guy tries to get her into bed. Sings her this stupid song about how cold it is outside. And, oh yeah, Red Skelton falls in the pool — he's the funny guy. Anyway, my new wife looks a lot like Esther...long legs, beautiful skin, lovely breasts."

I'm wondering what Grampa Rip would say about Randy. "This fella needs to have the inside of his head hosed out..." Something like that, probably.

"...legs long like Esther's, really narrow waist, nice

breasts like that, nice beautiful smile like that — except her hair…her hair is more thicker and curly blonde, golden blonde. You should see her in her Esther Williams swim suit. She has one, ya know. I bought one for her. I buy her everything. Did ya know. They like ya to buy stuff fer them. Nice stuff. They'll do anything for you if you buy them stuff. And praise their hair. They like that. You know what I'm sayin'?"

Oh, Gerty, I wish I was with you right now instead of this…this…

What Happened • Three

*Y*OUR FATHER *was showing everybody the car he borrowed. Proud of it, he was.*

"A brand-new '51 Buick, four-door sedan. One thousand, nine hundred and ninety-five bucks is what she cost!"

You remembered how worried was Horrors' face as you drove off skidding down the snow-packed street. You waved. Trying to say with the wave to Horrors not to worry. Everything will be all right with the car.

Your father driving off, never looking back.

Some of the neighbors were out in the street to say good-bye. Mrs. Laflamme was whispering to Mrs. Sawyer, "It's for the best. She hasn't been the same all this time — four or five years, is it? — since she lost the baby. And Phil is more and more of a burden...getting bigger and bigger...harder to handle!"

"And she gets absolutely no help at home..."

"It will be hard for a while but it's best in the long run..."

"It's very sad, it is."

Phil was in a good mood when you helped put him in the backseat. He had extra napkins on, in case. He had a rubber toy that squeaked when he squeezed. He showed it to you. His strange eyes. He has feelings, *you thought.*

Your mother was standing fussing with her clothes and her purse.

"Come on," your father was saying. "Hurry up and get in! The next time we take you anywhere we'll leave you at home!"

Your father couldn't wait to get driving Horrors' new car.

Cheap was in the living-room window, saying good-bye.

Mrs. Laflamme would feed him. Not to worry.

You drove off. It had started to snow. Big flakes. Mild weather.

"Snowstorm coming. Doesn't matter to us, though. Not in this machine! We're going to find Highway 15. Then it's straight down 15 to Smiths Falls! It's a long drive. So just sit back and relax!"

You drove through the thickening storm.

Phil was happy squeezing his rubber toy, making it squeak and giggling and bubbling.

Your father, taking a sip from his small rye bottle, was singing.

Your mother sat staring straight ahead. Your father

singing. Happy. Another sip of his rye: "There's no tomorrow...when love is true..."

Another sip.

"What a beautiful machine is this car!"

*Your father, the singer. They loved it in the tavern
when he sang. If they only knew what he was like at
home!*

"There's no tomorrow / There's just tonight!..."

9

Nine Pages

WE'RE ON Cobourg Street near where I used to live on Papineau. We go into Prevost's Lunch Room and Grocery where I used to go all the time when I was a kid with my friend Billy Batson. The ancient man is still sitting in the corner there in his highchair killing flies. I remember him. Hard to believe he's still alive. It's easy in the spring. These flies are very slow. They're not awake yet.

I'm a little surprised that Randy's not stealing from here but I don't say anything. Then we go down to the corner to St. Patrick Street Confectioners. Same thing.

Same thing happens in the other little store, Lachaine's. I used to go there on my way to school. It's right near Heney Park where an awful thing happened to me one time. A man named Mr. George hurt me there once. But that's over now.

"I've decided," says Randy, "since we're pals and everything now, I'm going to take you home to my place for lunch."

"Your place."

"Yep, I live right down there. Number 60 Cobourg Street, Apartment 403."

I look across at number three Papineau, the house where I used to live. And number five, where my hero Buz lived with his mother. And number seven where my friend Billy Batson used to live. And number one. Horseball Laflamme and his big family.

While Randy's talking to Mr. Lachaine I stroll down Cobourg Street to Papineau and try to look in the window of my old house, number three. I see a strange couch and a sad-looking table. A small airplane is droning in the sky over Lowertown. The sound of the droning plane makes me think of when I was a little kid, home from school, sick, lying in my mother's bed under the special comforter, sick with fever, wishing I was in that little plane going somewhere, anywhere, droning away, trailing my life behind me...

Randy's back.

"Bring your lunch up. We'll have lunch together."

The truck is parked at the back of 60 Cobourg Street, under the fire escape. It's a big brown apartment building with dirty windows.

We go in. A little elevator shakes while it takes us to the fourth floor. We go down the dark dirty hallway to his door beside the garbage chute.

There's a rusty nail in the door — probably to hang something on — a wreath at Christmas, maybe.

We go in and we're in the kitchen. There are dirty dishes all over the place and there's spilled food on the oilcloth floor.

"I want to show you something," Randy says. We go in the living room and Randy goes over to a book shelf that's filled mostly with magazines and old newspapers.

There's a folder on the top shelf beside a clock that is stopped and covered with dust. He takes it down and opens it. There are some pages, a bit yellow, with funny-looking typing on them.

"'Member I told you 'bout the Commie spy smasher, Igor? The Russians were gonna kill him because he squealed? Igor, who lived in yer apartment? Well, that night when he escaped, I stole these papers from a bag he had, a cloth bag with wooden handles. There's nine pages. All in funny letters. Probably Russian. Looks like lists or something. And some Ottawa places. And some Canadian names. I thought the papers would be worth something but Igor, he disappeared so...you know. You never know...might be worth something some day. Quite a coincidence, eh?"

He puts the folder back up beside the dusty clock.

Randy puts me back in the kitchen now. It's a mess. Dirty dishes. Leftover breakfast in the frying pan. Stained tablecloth. Sour milk in a milk bottle. Moldy cheese on the windowsill. Torn, dirty curtain.

Grampa Rip would be disgusted. "Are there bears livin' here?" he might say.

I sit at the table and set my brown lunch bag in front

of me. I've got pork sandwiches today. Pork and sweet mustard. But nothing to drink. I've had my one free drink for the day.

"Go down to the truck and get a Lemon 'N Lime for me and a Honee Orange for you."

"But I already had my drink for the day."

"Never mind that. Go! And when you come back sit by the window so you can look down and see the truck. Make sure no kids are around tryin' to steal drinks!"

Funny how crooks don't trust anybody.

I get back with the drinks and sit at the window and start eating my lunch while I'm watching the truck down there through the black iron fire escape.

The Honee Orange and the pork are good. And the sweet mustard.

Suddenly I see down there some kids around the truck. They are looking all around.

"I'm going down to the truck!" I shout. "There's kids going to steal!"

"Okay!" Randy shouts from the other room.

I go down and chase the kids. I tell them the driver is crazy and he has a gun. They run off.

I go back up the slow, shaky elevator.

I sit at the kitchen table with Randy.

"What do you think of Jews?" says Randy. This is going to be our lunch conversation.

"Jews? What do you mean, Jews?" I don't think anything about Jews.

"Do you know who Karl Marx is?"

"Does he work at Pure Spring?" I like to play dumb with Randy. Playing dumb makes me sort of invisible.

"No, dummy. Karl Marx is dead. A hundred years ago he dreamed up Communism. Karl Marx was a Jew. Jews with their crazy ideas. Why do you think Hitler tried to kill them all? He almost made it. You know why he hated them, tried to exterminate them?"

"Because he was crazy?"

"No, because he was a Christian."

I nearly choke on my Honee Orange at this last bit of wisdom.

"Yes, a Christian. A Christian who loved Jesus Christ. And who do you think killed Jesus Christ? The Jews killed Jesus Christ. Killed our Lord. And now the Commies are making religion illegal!"

I'm going to forget about trying to eat the rest of my lunch. I think I'd rather be having a lunch date with Adolf Hitler than Randy.

Randy's rolling.

"Did you know that in Communist Russia today, this very minute, while we're having this educational discussion..."

Educational discussion?

"...this educational discussion, if you are caught praying to God in Russia they stick a tube in your head and suck out your brains and feed them to the pigs?"

That's it. I'm going down to the truck.

"Where ya goin'?"

"I need some air."

"Having trouble with a little bit of reality there, sissy? Boy O'Boy with the fancy Latin words. There's lots you don't know."

"Where's your wife?" I say, surprising myself.

There's a long pause. He's looking out the window. I'm heading out the door.

"She's gone shopping," he says.

Up the street in Heney Park there are couples strolling, hand in hand, stopping from time to time to kiss. In the spring.

The redwing blackbirds are sounding like referee's whistles.

Oh, Gerty!

I have to tell you everything but I'm afraid.

And Grumpa Rip, too. Tell him. What will he think of me?

10

Gerty and the Pork Hock

THE TREES are exploding. If you look at a tree and look away and look back, it's already bigger!

Gerty and I are on the streetcar. People are dressed up. It's Sunday. The sun is shining, the birds are chasing each other and chirping through the bushes, the church bells are ringing, people are sweeping and cleaning and the clothes on the clotheslines are dancing.

I rode my bicycle over to her place. We're taking the streetcar back to my place. Then we'll take the streetcar back to her place and then I'll ride my bicycle back to my place. Busy, busy, busy!

Even the streetcar conductor is whistling and humming a tune. Gerty and I know what it is. It's "Because of You" by Tony Bennett. The streetcar conductor isn't Tony Bennett. But that's all right. I do a little imitation of Tony Bennett (you sing high is how you do it): "Because of you the sun will shine…Forever…"

But my voice is too low and it cracks. Gerty laughs. I love the way she laughs.

She's wearing the little straw hat with the robin's-egg-blue ribbon and the rosebud-shaped bow.

Blue is her favorite color. A lot of her clothes are blue.

Outside my apartment there are two chickadees fighting over the hairs I stuck in the screen of our round bathroom window.

"That's a good idea. I'm going to try that. My hair is quite long so when I brush it there are good strong long hairs for nest building stuck in the brush," says Gerty.

I know, Gerty. I could build a nest out of your hair and live in it the rest of my life, I almost say but I don't.

The apartment is warm because the oil furnace is still on. I hang up my jacket. Gerty has on a pullover sweater.

"I think I'll take this off," she says. "Hold down my blouse at the back."

I hold the bottom of her blue silk blouse at the back so it won't come up with the sweater while she pulls it over her head. Then she shakes her hair out, smooths down the front of her blouse and straightens out her blue ribbon.

"There," she says and looks at me as much as to say, How do I look, and I fall into her eyes and drown myself there.

I bring her into the living room and we see Grampa Rip from the back in his huge rocking chair.

Gerty is looking around like she just walked into a

giant's museum. She's looking up at Grampa Rip's very large painting of the Virgin Mary and her son. The Virgin Mary is dressed in blue.

The chair moves and Cheap jumps off and then Grampa gets out. He's all dressed and ready to go to another funeral wake at McEvoy's. We're going to go, too. But lunch, first.

"How do you do, miss," he says to Gerty and takes her hand in his big fingers. "I'm pleased to report that we're having pork hocks and fried potatoes for lunch on this lovely spring day!"

I'm a little embarrassed because I think that maybe somebody as beautiful and delicate and feminine as Gerty would be horrified at the big fat ankle of a pig covered with thick bristly tough skin squatting on a plate in front of her like a swollen toad.

"I like pork hock," says Gerty. "My grampa makes the best pork hock in Sandy Hill. And he used to pickle them but since Gramma died…"

I can tell Grampa Rip likes her already.

"Well, young miss, you'll have to be very frank with me during lunch and compare your grandfather's hock with mine!"

While Gerty helps me set the table Grampa talks at the stove over the boiling hocks and frying potatoes with onions.

"You know, you have the same name as a famous figure in literature. Gerty McDowell. In James Joyce's great novel *Ulysses*, a very large whack of an important chapter is dedicated to her. And I must say your appearance is remarkably similar!"

"I'll try to read that book one day, Mr. Sawyer. There's so much to read and so little time."

"HA! HA! HA!" shouts Grampa Rip, letting the laughter rip. "You've got plenty of time...plenty of time before it's over. But I'll tell you one thing for sure. You may look like Gerty McDowell but you very certainly aren't like her in any way. No. In the book, our Gerty would never eat a pork hock. She's a little too prissy for that. Not like you!"

I'm starting to get jealous, Grampa Rip and Gerty are getting along so well.

But it's okay. Because now we're kicking each other under the table, Gerty and me.

Peel the floppy skin off the pork hock and place it politely on the side of your plate. Strip some of the delicious lean meat with your fork, dip it in the hot mustard. Eat it. Wash it down with a mouthful of fried potatoes and onions. Don't be afraid to swallow some fat with it.

Gerty knows exactly how.

We step out of the apartment building. People up and down Somerset Street are washing their cars and changing their storm windows and sweeping their walks and oiling their bicycles.

The Gray Man sits on the bench under the exploding maple tree. There are baby carriages and kids playing ball and marbles in the mud and old men sucking on pipes in the spring sun.

On our way to the funeral wake I tell Gerty a little bit about the Gray Man and the Russians and the Communists and Igor Gouzenko and how he lived in our apartment and how famous he was and how my boss Randy lived across the hall from him when the Russian agents tried to capture and kill Igor, and I tell a bit about Randy. But not all. Too embarrassing.

I tell about some of the names of some of the stores we sell drinks to. I mention Persephone's Grocery. She says shyly, "That's Greek mythology. I love Greek mythology. Persephone — she's the daughter of Demeter, the goddess of corn, of food, really — she was taken, kidnapped by Hades and forced to go to the underworld to be his queen but then she was allowed to come back once each year for a while. She's the radiant maiden of the spring!..."

And Grampa Rip, who is walking in front of us, turns around and says big and loud so that everybody around on Kent Street looks over and with his arms out he shouts, "And her light step makes the brown hillside fresh and blooming and sets the tiny lambs on wobbly legs!"

And then Gerty claps her hands, applauding.

We're in front of McEvoy's funeral home.

"Maybe we won't go in with you this time, Grampa Rip. Maybe next time. We'll take a walk and then I'll go home on the streetcar with Gerty..."

Grampa Rip with his face says he understands.

"Have a nice time, Mr. Sawyer!" Gerty shouts as he goes up the stairs. "Oh my God," she says, covering her mouth. "What did I say? What did I say? He's going into a funeral home and I say have a nice time…oh, why did I say that?"

"You said it just right," I say. "He always has a good time at funerals. That's why he goes. You said it just right."

We stroll along in the warm, luscious, springtime sunshine.

A man in a laneway is washing his kid's little wagon with a hose. He's got his radio plugged in on the veranda.

The radio is playing the Hit Parade.

Gerry puts her hand inside my hand.

"I think you're so lucky to have a grampa like Grampa Rip. He's so smart and funny and kind."

The radio plays the first note of "Too Young" by Nat "King" Cole. It's kind of a BOINNG! kind of sound. It's an all-of-a-sudden sort of sound. A springtime sound. A Gerty McDowell sound.

That's what happens to my whole body when Gerty puts her hand inside my hand.

It's an all-of-a-sudden kind of BOINNG! kind of feeling.

Today after lunch, while we were cleaning up the dishes, Gerty told Grampa Rip that his pork hocks were just as good as her grampa's used to be but her grampa's aren't as good any more because he's so sick and sad all the time…

There was a long silent piece of time. Only the dishes making noise.

Then a conversation took place that was surprising to Gerty but not to me. Not if you know Grampa Rip like I do.

Grampa Rip: Your Grampa McDowell. What's his first name?

Gerty: Mutt. His real name's Matthew but his friends call him Mutt.

Grampa Rip: I think I know him. Is he from up the Gatineau? Low? Kazabazua?

Gerty: Kazabazua.

Grampa Rip: Mutt McDowell. I know him. I met him workin' on the Parliament Buildings after the Centre Block burnt in 1915. It was 1916 and he was back from the Big War. One of the lucky ones. Got gassed by the Germans at Ypres in Belgium. Many, many Canadians were slaughtered. But they held the line. Mutt was a hero.

Gerty: Yes, that's him. He was a hero. Now he's very sick.

Grampa Rip: Gassed by chlorine gas in a muddy ditch and for what?

Gerty: Poor Grampa! The floorboards used to creak in his kitchen when he walked on them. Now they don't creak, he's so small, so light.

Grampa Rip: A fine man in his day. A witty man. A good man. Raising the Union Jack because they thought the enemy had surrendered. But it was a trick. "Gas! Gas!" the soldiers yelled and scrambled for their gas masks.

Gerty: He never told us about it.

Grampa Rip: They don't like to talk about it. Sometimes they wish they'd died alongside their comrades. Wasted away after being ruined in a ditch in some foreign country just to satisfy some egotistical, evil old bastards

calling themselves generals, who died peacefully in bed
of old age while Mutt goes around for years only half
able to breathe…

Gerty: Oh, Grampa Rip (crying), it's so sad!

Grampa Rip: The old lie. *Dulce et decorum est pro patria
mori.* Lovely and honorable it is to die for one's country. Wilfred Owen, poet.

Grampa Rip stopped and gripped the sink, his back
turned so we wouldn't see his tears.

Grampa Rip (turning to us): But youth will save us. Save
us old sad ones. You, Gerty, I'm sure, are a great com-
fort to Mutt. And I'll tell you something. I, too, was
sad for quite a while but I'm not any more. The reason
for that is my young friend here, Martin O'Boy. He has
brought back my happiness by his presence here.

Our Bank streetcar turns up Queen Street and then
down past the Union Station. Couples are hugging and
crying and laughing in front of the station as usual.
Leaving and coming home. Coming home and leaving.

I see across the street the doorman at the Chateau
Laurier in his spring uniform admiring how white his
white gloves are. Look at my gloves. Look at me! It's
spring!

I look at Gerty. She sees him, too.

11
Not the Time

TONIGHT WE'RE going to the show. The Capitol Theatre. *A Streetcar Named Desire* is what's playing. There's a big line-up right around the block. People in the line-up are talking about how some parts of the movie were censored. There were parts that were too sexy and so people weren't allowed to see them.

Gerty has a much larger blue ribbon tying her hair.

People in the line-up are saying you have to be eighteen to get in. Guy behind us says he's only seventeen but he's seen the movie three times.

"This is the fourth time I'll see it," he says.

Gerty gives me a look. The look says it all. Does he really have to tell us that? We can add. Three times plus one time is four times. Some people.

"This bigger ribbon makes me look older, don't you think?" Gerty says to me.

I want to kiss the ribbon.

Maybe I'll tell her tonight during the movie. Tell her all

about stealing from her store. Tell her in the dark. Easier, maybe, that way. Won't see my eyes. My shame.

I'm wearing a white shirt and one of Grampa Rip's ties.

"Do you think this tie makes me look older?"

"I don't know. We'll have to wait and see." Then she says, "Exciting, isn't it?"

When we're about fourth from the front of the line I can tell by the look on the face of the lady in the box office that she's too tired to be bothered asking about how old we are.

When it's our turn I speak right into the round hole in the window in a low, very serious voice, "Two adults, if you please," and slap my dollar bill on the marble surface with what Grampa Rip would call Authority.

She slides the two tickets over and the change — thirty cents — comes jingling out of the cash register down a slide and into the silver container.

"We're all adults tonight, sonny," she says. She sounds like she's just about ready to drop dead from boredom.

Gerty is imitating me as we float through the huge lobby leading to the stairs. "If you please..." she's saying, trying to do a low voice.

The lobby is decorated with carved frames and columns that look like marble and the ceiling is made of panels of gold and cream and rose red and the walls are decorated with flowers in plaster and brightly painted vases and cornices of fruits and foliage and animals and dancing figures in patterns and swirls and flowing lines and strange scenes like in a dream.

Then the two royal curving staircases and the sweeping banisters with hundreds of little pillars fat at the bottom and the huge high domed ceiling. You look up, up, and don't forget to breathe!

Along the walls are arches and hiding places and pillars and caves over the doorways and tapestries and carvings heavy with grapes and buds and hanging apples and palm trees.

There are naked fairies dancing in the woods, monsters peeking, creatures — half man half tree, half woman half fish — and bare-ass children playing horns and fiddles and throwing flowers and seashells at each other.

And then the heavy drapes and stuffed sofas of rich cloth, velvet and velour and your feet sinking into the old, thick, soft, rose-red carpet.

Then, in the theater where the seats are, the magnificent chandelier hanging down from the sunburst dome begins to dim and the hundreds of hidden lights glittering from everywhere begin to fade and now only the spotlights on the heavy curtain are left and now the curtain swooping open and all lights are out now and the music starts and the crowd of a thousand people hushes and the previews for the upcoming movies begin.

A perfect magic palace. A perfect place to tell the beautiful, magical girl you are with that you are a liar and a thief.

In *A Streetcar Named Desire* Marlon Brando plays Stanley. Stanley slaps his wife Stella and she runs away crying to the neighbor's house but then they make up and

Stella loves him more than ever. Everybody's poor and Stanley usually goes around in a torn, filthy T-shirt.

Then Stella's sister Blanche comes to stay and she insults Stanley, calling him a common pig which is what he is. But Stanley gets back at Blanche when he finds out that she has lied about her so-called fancy life in the past as a schoolteacher when all she really was was a sort of prostitute.

Blanche goes crazy because Stanley is so cruel to her and in the end everybody hates everybody and they cart old Blanche off to the loony bin.

Everybody in the Capitol Theatre is bawling like babies and Gerty is looking pretty sad, too, although she's not crying.

I hate this movie. It reminds me too much of my house — people throwing dishes and slapping wives across the face.

It's impossible to try and tell Gerty now.

12

This Time

THE RAT HOLE theater on Bank Street is really the Rialto but everybody calls it the Rat Hole because they say that when you sit there in the dark you can feel the rats jumping around your ankles fighting for the popcorn and candy on the floor down there.

It's not like the Capitol at all. There are maybe two steps up from the lobby, there are no rugs, no thick curtains. There are maybe two angels playing harps on the walls. The place smells of stinky feet, BO, perfume and popcorn.

Grampa Rip's friend Kelly O'Kelly is taking the tickets. Like Grampa Rip told me to do, I tell Kelly O'Kelly that Grampa Rip says hello and right away O'Kelly gives us back our tickets.

"Go right in," he says. "Save your tickets for next time you come."

Gerty likes going to the show with me even though that's two nights in a row now.

This is the Marx Brothers night. There are three Marx Brothers movies on: *A Night at the Opera*, *A Day at the Races* and *Horse Feathers*.

A Night at the Opera is very funny.

Groucho, Chico and Harpo and about fifteen other people are all crammed into a small bedroom on board a ship. Groucho has a date with the fat lady he's always insulting named Mrs. Claypool.

When she knocks on the door, Groucho, who is playing a crooked businessman named Otis B. Driftwood, says, "Come in!"

She opens the door and everybody falls out of the room on top of her.

I decide, because everybody's in such a good mood, to tell her.

At the end of the movie a whole lot of cops are chasing Groucho, Chico and Harpo during the performance of an opera. Of course, the opera is ruined and all the people at the Rat Hole are laughing their heads off while the opera singers are trying to sing and the sets come crashing down around them.

The next movie will be on in a minute and I ask Gerty if she wants to come out to the lobby with me to get some popcorn.

While we're walking up the aisle I start talking about Randy and how he has all of these schemes for stealing from our customers.

The more I tell her, the more confused her face gets.

Now we're leaving the show.

Now we're on the street.

Now we're on the streetcar.

I'm telling Gerty more about Randy now and how he steals. I can't help it. I'm getting closer. I tell about the scheme at Persephone's to get the guy to pay for more cases than he actually got. I tell that Randy has many schemes for many different stores.

Gerty has a storm coming over her face.

"Many stores?"

"Yes. Many. Many stores."

The streetcar conductor is banging his foot on the bell trying to get rid of a kid on a bicycle who's hitching a ride hanging on to the open back window.

"Did he steal from our store?"

The bell stops. The streetcar moves.

"Yes."

"Did you help him?"

"Yes. I did. I helped him."

Now, tears.

"You're not a thief. I know you. You're not a thief! Martin! Tell me you're not."

"I was. I *did* help. But he made me. I'd be fired if I didn't. No. It's not like that. You were our first store. It was after that I stole. When I was in your cellar I didn't realize what I was doing until it was over. Then I saw you."

"You're not a crooked stealing thief person. I know you!" says Gerty.

"How do you know me? You don't know anything about me."

"Can you get back what he made you steal? My gram-pa's losing money in the store."

"Maybe. I have a kind of plan."

"A kind of plan?"

"Yes. An almost plan."

"When you have that plan, Martin O'Boy, come and see me and tell me what it is."

She kisses me light on the cheek, her fingers on my shoulder, her lips brushing right above the corner of my mouth on the left side.

"Don't come and see me ever again unless you have that plan. The plan to get back what was stolen from us."

I get off the streetcar at my stop.

She says she knows me. How does she know me? How can she say she knows me? Nobody knows me. Nobody in this world knows me.

The streetcar pulls away. She's in her seat, staring straight ahead. She doesn't glance at me standing there.

13

Everything Reminds

GRAMPA RIP asks me why Gerty didn't come back after that one visit and then he pauses a bit. Then he says I don't have to tell him if I don't want to. And then he says, "Be careful, Martin, my young friend. It's spring and 'In the spring a young man's fancy lightly turns to thoughts of love.' That's by Tennyson, a fine poet!"

Then he says I'll feel better if I write it down. How I feel.

I'm sitting at the secretariat writing in the notebook Grampa gave to me — writing about Gerty, mostly how beautiful she is and how just about everything I see and hear and smell and touch and taste reminds me of her.

Cheap, half asleep, watches me write. He likes to see the pencil moving up and down along the page and now and then sometimes he puts his furry little hand out and touches gentle the place where the pencil is pressing the paper. And he likes, I think, the warm coming from the secretariat's writing light.

I'm also working on my theft list. Every night I record

what Randy and I are stealing. The store. The time. The way we did it. The amount of money we are stealing: almost one hundred dollars a week! I have it all written down right from that first day at McDowell's Grocery and Lunch on Sweetland Avenue.

Grampa's huge painting of the Pieta — the Virgin Mary with the dead body of Jesus across her legs — reminds me of Gerty. The Virgin is wearing the same color blue that is Gerty's favorite color.

I wish that was Gerty in the painting and that was me she was crying over.

Everything reminds me of her.

Grampa Rip has a bird feeder hanging outside our round bathroom window. He has a book on the windowsill called *Birds of Ottawa*. You can look in the book and name the different birds that visit. The chickadees, nuthatches, goldfinches, cardinals, redpolls and bluejays all remind me of Gerty.

Last Sunday I went with Grampa Rip to one of his funeral wakes. Grampa had a nice time at the wake talking to some old people he met near the coffin who knew somebody who knew somebody else that he knew once. A nice time. That reminded me of Gerty. Even the flowers around the dead body reminded me of Gerty.

A kid pushing a little wagon reminds me of Gerty. The leaves on the trees that used to be buds remind me of Gerty. Streetcars remind me of Gerty. The doorman at the Chateau Laurier reminds me of Gerty. His white gloves.

A butterfly, a silver buckle, a robin's egg. A straw hat,

panties in the window of A.J. Freiman's department store remind me of Gerty. Nat "King" Cole singing "Too Young" reminds me of Gerty. Maple syrup, clouds, running water, violins, hairs in a hairbrush, rain, pianos, ice cream cones, my cat Cheap, cocoa, the sound of the oil furnace, a foggy windowpane. Habitant soup, Honee Orange, dinging and donging of bells, milkshakes and hamburgers, ribbons, lilacs and *Konk-a-ree! Konk-a-ree!* all remind me of Gerty.

I'm imitating a redwing blackbird saying Gerty's name. It's the middle of the night.

Konk-Gertee! Konk-Gertee!

Cheap is looking at me. Am I crazy?

Grampa Rip comes out in his long pajama gown and his cap with the tassel hanging over his ear.

"Did I wake you up? I'm sorry," I tell him.

"I always get up with the birds," he says, "but redesigned blackbirds in the middle of the night?"

Grampa Rip looks over my shoulder at what I'm writing. I try to cover my theft pages but he sees.

"Keeping books? Bookkeeping. Always wise to keep track of your money. Every cent counts. It all adds up. Every penny, every nickel, every dime. Can get to be a pretty big pile one day! I know from experience."

He goes around and sits in his giant rocker. Cheap jumps up on his lap.

You can't fool Grampa Rip. You can't hide from Grampa Rip. You can't pretend or lie to Grampa Rip. You have to tell.

And it's okay to tell.

Because you know that Grampa Rip will never turn on you, yell at you, say you're stupid, say you're wrong, say you shouldn't have done that, say you should be ashamed of yourself, say you're no good, say you're a waste of time, say you'll never amount to anything in this world, say you should never have been born...

I bring my notebook around to the front of Grampa Rip's giant rocking chair with the two wooden eagles and I sit on the rug and I tell him everything about the stealing. About Randy and the birth certificate. About day number one and Mutt McDowell's six stolen cases of drinks.

There's a long silence after I'm finished.

"The birth certificate. It's safe?"

I pull out my wallet and show him the priceless plastic-covered document. His eyes are full on me.

"Good lad!" he says. "Show me more?"

I do. I show him each bookkeeping page. Each day. Each theft.

"Very interesting," says Grampa Rip. "A series of serious crimes. And a Romance Interruptus. I take it that Miss G. McDowell now wants no part of you because she believes you to be a thief and your heart is now broken hearted."

He winks at me. I know he's teasing me. I say what he expects me to say.

"Your heart can't be broken hearted. Either your heart is broken or *you* are broken hearted. It is *redundant* to say your heart is broken hearted..."

BRIAN DOYLE

"You learn well, Martin O'Boy. Now. After we get
some sleep we'll be more fresh and able to decide what to
do with this thieving, blackmailing, bullying specimen.
And then maybe, just maybe, we can get the lovely Gerty
McDowell back for another pork hock!"

To bed. Oh, yes. When I told Grampa Rip all about
Randy and the wedding pictures and about Randy the
roofer and Randy the vacuum cleaner salesman and Randy
this and Randy that, he said a very funny thing. He said,
"This Randy fella, somebody should hose out that brain
pan of his with an industrial-strength disinfectant!"

Cheap, purring away beside me, reminds me of Gerty.
My pillow reminds me of Gerty.

The last Somerset streetcar of the night goes rumbling
by; a mouse scratches between the walls; the creak of the
back stairs that lead from the yard to our back balcony —
somebody coming home late; the sound of someone near
our back kitchen door; the smell of my own hand; the
place on my cheek where she — right above the corner of
my mouth on the left side — brushed her lips and the very
same place on my shoulder where she put her fingers…all
remind me…

Go to sleepy, Gerty, sleep…

Rat-tat-tat-tat-tat! Five times on our back door. Loud.
Sharp. Never heard this around here half asleep before.
Knuckles on the door. Hard on the door. Important.

Five *rat-tat-tats* again. I fumble out of bed. Cheap hits
the floor with his two soft thumps.

We all — Grampa Rip, Cheap and me — get to the kitchen door at the same time. Turn on the light.

The door is opening. It's now open.

A man standing straight as a board. A man with a thick neck, not too tall, a large chin, a straight mouth, square head, turned-up nose, baggy suit, heavy accent, raises one eyebrow and says, "Allow me to introduce myself. I am Igor Gouzenko, Russian defector and famous Canadian hero! May I come in?"

"Grampa Rip," I whisper. "He used to live here!"

"Correct, young man!" says Igor.

"Come in," says Grampa Rip. "Come in and be welcome!"

What Happened • Four

*Y*OU STOPPED *at a restaurant in the town of Carleton Place. The restaurant was called Bellamy's. It was on the main street. Bridge Street.*

It was in there that Phil all of a sudden decided to throw his lemon meringue pie all over the place — on the table, on our faces, on the floor, on the next table, on the wall and even over a huge man sitting on a stool at the counter.

The restaurant had booths along the wall with little nickelodeons in each booth and six stools with red leather seats along a counter on the other side. In a glass case there were huge pies — apple, blueberry, lemon meringue.

There were two people at the counter. One on stool number one. One on stool number six.

They were far apart but they knew each other.

The man was a very large farmer, so large you couldn't see the stool he was sitting on. The lady at the other end was thin and straight and had a high raspy voice.

"Big storm comin'," she said.

"Here already," the huge farmer said.

He had lemon meringue pie on his back.

The waitress rushed over to our table.

You heard the waitress whisper, whisper, whisper to your mother.

"Don't worry. It's all right. I understand. I have one at home myself. Everything's going to be just fine," the waitress said.

You wondered about the word. One.

One.

I have one at home.

One what? One boy just like Phil.

You wondered, was it true there were other boys, people in the world just like Phil?

"How is it," you heard your mother ask. "How is it that you are able to leave yours at home while you're out? I can't go anywhere or leave him with anybody the way he is."

"I'm lucky," you heard the kind waitress say. She was cleaning off the table and wiping lemon meringue pie off Phil's head. You saw Phil calming down when the waitress spoke soft to him. She rubbed Phil's back and she talked quiet to your mother. You saw.

"My husband's a fireman. Works in the city," she said. "He has lots of time off in the daytime. Works nights a lot. Takes care of Junior so I can do some shifts here. Bellamy's — good people to work for."

"You're lucky, all right," your mother whispered so your father wouldn't hear. He was fiddling with the little nickelodeon. Looking in his pockets for a nickel. "You're lucky to have the help. I have no help. I can't go anywhere. This is my first real trip since he was born. Hard to believe but they're twins, you know."

The kind waitress looked at you. Her eyes said she almost didn't believe it.

"Oh!" she said. Then she changed the subject. "Oh. Where are you going on your trip?"

"Oh, just a drive to Smiths Falls to see some relatives."

"Watch out for the storm coming," the waitress said.

"Here already," the huge farmer with the lemon meringue pie on his back said.

"We have a good car," your father said. He put a nickel in the nickelodeon. "Brand new as a matter of fact. Latest thing for the snow. Special snow tires! What'll they think of next, eh?"

When the waitress turned her back your father poured rye whiskey into the water in his water glass. The water in the glass was now gold colored.

You had hot chicken sandwiches and French fried potato chips. With salt and vinegar.

Your father kept playing the same song: "Put another nickel in/In the nickelodeon."

Phil started pouring vinegar on his ruined lemon pie. You took the vinegar bottle away from him, gentle, and Phil looked at you with his strange eyes.

You were together since you were born.

"Let him if he wants," your father said. "What's the difference? Vinegar on lemon pie? Could taste real good depending on who you are. I'm not gonna try it though. Not this Canadian. Not this time around! HA! HA!"

Loud, so's the others in the restaurant would hear.

Phil started throwing his head around and almost howling. It was time to go. You had to leave some of your hot chicken sandwich (the gravy was getting sticky glue cold anyway).

You helped Phil with his winter coat and hat and out you went.

You knew Phil would be better in the car, would calm down because of the sound of the engine. Phil also liked the hypnotizing snow coming at us. He dozed off. Your strange twin.

"I couldn't tell that woman where we were taking Phil," your mother said in the front seat. "Couldn't bring myself to tell her."

"So?" your father said. "It's none of her business. She's a stranger. What we do has nothing to do with some waitress in a two-bit village!"

Your father was yelling.

"She has help," your mother said. "Help to deal, day in and day out, with the one she has!"

"There's no help for this! Let's get it done and over with. Over and done with!"

More hypnotizing snow.

"And anyway, a fireman? All they do is sleep all night in the fire station and get paid for it. No wonder he has so much time!"

Phil snoring a little bit. Silence for a while.

"They should be paid only if there's a fire! That'd be good, wouldn't it?"

Your mother quiet again.

"Paid by the fire. That's a good one!"

You thought your father had not heard the whispering but he had.

"But then again, if they were paid by the fire, they'd probably *be out at night settin' the fires just so's they'd get paid! Ha! Ha! Ha!"*

You wished you were somewhere else. Anywhere else.

14

Moths and Flames

"WHAT A wonderful thing it is, Mr. Gouzenko," Grampa Rip is saying, "that we live in the very same apartment that you did. What a great honor it is. You are a great man!"

"Enough!" says Mr. Gouzenko. "The honor is mine! You are too generous. I come for nostalgic. For memory of old days!"

"Of course. Welcome! Come into the living room and sit down. I'll put on the kettle! Better still, Martin, will you put on the kettle like a good lad?"

"Is grandson?..."

"Well, yes and no..."

In the kitchen I can hear the talking back and forward. When Grampa Rip asks me to put the kettle on he really wants me to make tea. I put on the kettle and get out the cups and the milk and sugar.

Might as well put out some bread and butter while I'm at it. Maybe slice up some cold roast pork and set a jar of hot mustard and some pickles and salt and pepper on the table. And the homemade applesauce and there's some potato salad left over from supper...

While I'm doing this I try to listen in to what they are saying. Some of it is about me. Grampa Rip is telling Igor about how I came to live with him and how I felt so small when I first came here, and how the doctor said that a big boy like I was shouldn't be feeling so small and that I'd better not be going to school in such a condition — have to feel big again before I'd go back.

"He was pretty sick when he first came here," Grampa Rip says, "but he's a lot better now."

Now Igor is talking about how he'll never, ever see his parents again. He's heard his mother is ill and he can't communicate with her. They will never see him again. To lose your parents. Very sad.

Now there's a long silence.

A silence to be sad in.

A strange man this Mr. Gouzenko.

The first thing he did when we brought him in was he fell face first to the kitchen floor and did ten pushups with only his fingertips touching. Inside his baggy suit his body was straight and stiff as a steel beam.

And when Grampa introduced me to him and while I shook his powerful hand, he held it a little longer, looked in my eyes and said, "Ah! A young man in love!"

How did he know that? There must be pictures of Gerty McDowell in my eyes.

The kitchen table looks good with the huge wooden

legs carved like giant bowling pins holding up the tea and the pork and the potato salad.

Grampa brings Mr. Gouzenko back into the kitchen. He's carrying Cheap. They've made friends. Cheap doesn't make friends that fast, usually. Igor Gouzenko must be a nice man. He's stroking Cheap's head.

"Where is ear?" he asks Cheap. "You are like Russian cat. Communists take other ear?"

While we eat, Mr. Gouzenko keeps lifting up his teacup to click it against ours. Toasting.

Grampa Rip and Mr. Gouzenko can't stop talking about everything. What it was like right after the war when he lived here with his wife Svetlana and his little boy. And when he exposed the spies in Canada and how the Russians, his countrymen, tried to kill him.

How he escaped with his family. Then they talk about the old days before the war on the farm, how Grampa Rip's old-time farming in Canada was almost exactly the same as Igor Gouzenko's was back in Russia. How they had no telephones, no electricity, no tractors, only horses, and how hard they worked and what fun they had.

And while we are finishing eating, Mr. Gouzenko looks at his watch and points to our radio on top of the icebox.

"May I turn on radio?"

Then he fiddles around the dial until he finds what he wants.

"Toronto Symphony," he says. "Tonight Tchaikovsky!" And soon the radio has a huge orchestra with every instrument playing, and Igor Gouzenko is standing at the table waving his arms like an important conductor, conducting our radio on the icebox.

While Mr. Gouzenko conducts the radio, Grampa Rip goes up high in the kitchen cupboard and takes down a bottle of whiskey.

"Ah, Jameson!" says Igor. "My favorite! After vodka, of course!" And now everybody's laughing and the radio's back being off and Grampa and Igor are talking about the good old days without electricity and Igor is saying something about moths...

"The moths, at night. Before lightbulbs, only flames in lamps. Moths must be careful. Fly around flames. Dangerous." He's looking at me. "Too close to flame, wings get burnt up. Must be careful!"

"Our friend is talking about the moth and the flame, Martin. Young love. Dangerous. 'Thus hath the candle singed the moth. O, these deliberate fools!'" says Grampa.

"Poetry! To poetry!" says Igor, and up go the glasses again.

"Man who loves poetry is man I trust. You have education. Is good! You go to university when young?" Igor asks Grampa Rip.

"University! No, I didn't go to school at all! Not for long, anyway. Just long enough to learn to read and write. But my grandfather, Hack Sawyer, set me on the road to learning. He showed me how to educate myself while working. I had many, many jobs that required no brain at all. Hack showed me how to memorize poems while digging a ditch. How to read great novels while I ate my lunch. How to study the encyclopedia while standing on an assembly line with the other robots! Hack Sawyer was a genius!"

I'm proud of Grampa Rip, how he explains to Igor about his past.

And now, about Igor.

He lives somewhere with his family in Canada. A secret. Nobody must know. Dangerous for him and his family. The Russians still want to hurt him.

And now they are talking about danger and how dangerous it was for Igor that night and other nights when the Russians were looking for him and they would have killed him if they'd found him because he told Canada how many spies they had spying in Ottawa for the Communists.

And Igor tells how to protect yourself if you're in danger.

"Distract, then act! Distract, then act," Igor says. "Just like in nature. Do what mother partridge does when fox comes too close to nest. *Pretend* to be wounded and limp away. Fox will follow. Then when fox is far from nest — fly to safety."

Now quiet. Now glasses raised.

Really quiet now.

Igor leans closer to the table.

We all do. Lean in. Heads close. Something coming.

"I have confession to make," he says.

It's 3:00 A.M. in the morning. Everything is so quiet. Even the oil furnace isn't saying anything.

"I am not here for nostalgic, memory of old days. I apologize. I lie. But now I trust you. I tell you truth."

Mr. Gouzenko tells us about that night. How the Russians broke down his door. Our door. How he hid in another neighbor's apartment. How he escaped. How he came back. How he gave papers in English to the police. How the government moved his family. How he became a Canadian hero. How he still lives in a secret place somewhere in Canada. How he needs money.

"...and why come back here?" Grampa whispers.

"To get something. Something valuable. Something I can sell for money for my family."

"Something?"

"Papers. Papers in Russian language."

"Where?"

"Here. In apartment in floor."

"Where? What floor?"

"In bedroom."

We go into the bedroom.

"Under bed."

Under the bed is Grampa's strongbox. We move the big bed. We slide the box out from the wall. Igor is almost as strong as both the movers Frankie *and* Johnny.

With Grampa Rip's hammer and crowbar we take up some floor boards.

There's a cloth bag with wood handles. Igor takes it carefully up and opens it. He takes out a handful of papers tied with a cloth ribbon. He unties the ribbon. Flips through the papers.

He looks up. His face is tight.

"Important pages missing. Nine pages. Package is not worth much money without complete pages. Rare historical documents to sell to archives. I need money. For my family. I am discouraged. Almost worthless unless complete."

My mind is a merry-go-round. Randy's place. A dirty book shelf filled with old newspapers and magazines. A dusty, stopped clock. A folder on the top shelf.

There's something fluttering its wings inside me. These words come out of my throat like spring birds chirping.

"I know where those missing pages are."

Have I grown another head?

You'd think so, the way Igor and Grampa Rip are staring at me.

15

Sandy and Strawberry

TRUCK NUMBER 15 is on Sussex Street. Number 24. It's the prime minister's house. Prime Minister Louis St. Laurent. He just moved in with his wife. Randy tells me that all prime ministers will stay in this fancy mansion from now on. Randy can't wait to get in the house, figure out a way to steal from the prime minister of Canada.

"They'll have lotsa parties here. Need a lotta soft drinks. To mix with their hard drinks. Get it? Soft? Hard?"

Yes, Randy. I get it. Very funny.

We pull into the circular driveway. There's a big black shiny car in front of us. A distinguished old man gets out.

"It's him!" says Randy and piles out of the truck and rushes over and sticks out his hand for the prime minister to shake.

"You may deliver the ginger ale at the rear of the house, young man. We're having a house warming! And best wishes to you and yours," says Prime Minister St. Laurent. He has a beautiful voice and hardly any French accent and a kind face. His blue suit is pressed perfect. He stands very straight. He sounds very wise.

We deliver the six cases of ginger ale around the back to a man in the kitchen with a white hat on.

I'm back in the truck thinking about Mr. Igor Gouzenko and how disappointed he was about the missing papers. He was even more discouraged when I told him who had the papers. He said he remembered Randy and knew what a crook he was because he was caught twice stealing cigarettes from Smitty's Smoke Shop and he said that if Randy ever found out that the papers were valuable he'd never give them back.

He said he'd take the cloth bag full of documents back home with him and that he trusted us not to tell. He was going home to think things over. He left a post office box number and a fake name in case we wanted to write him a letter. We laughed when he told us his fake name — Mr. John Smith.

My mind is very busy thinking about Gerty and what she said to me. Where she kissed me. I'm also very tired.

Discouraged, disappointed. Igor was...off into the night he went. Sleepy...not much sleep...Igor...

Suddenly Randy's back!

"Hey, wake up Mr. Sleepy Brain! Couldn't figure a way to get by the guy with the white hat. Maybe next time. Picked up this, though. Sitting right on the kitchen counter. Pretty snazzy, eh?"

He shows me a silver table cigarette lighter shaped like a beaver with CANADA engraved on the beaver's tail.

"This is going to look real snazzy on my mantelpiece, right, Boy?"

I'm wondering if maybe everything in Randy's apartment is stolen.

I'm so tired I can hardly stand up.

Back home after work now and it takes a minute or two for it to dawn on me that Grampa Rip's not here.

Lost again.

I go down to the corner of Somerset and Bank.

In front of Fenton's Bakery there's a small crowd. It's Sandy, Grampa Rip's friend who brought him home, putting on a show.

Sandy marches everywhere he goes. He learned to march in the war. His army uniform is khaki colored and there's a stripe on his shoulder. He marches all over the city every day. People sometimes give him money. But it's mostly food people give him. The breadman might give him a loaf of yesterday's bread or sometimes the milkman decides to give him a pint of milk if the bottle has a little chip out of the top of it or the vegetable man will give him a turnip or a couple of carrots or a big onion and once I saw a grocery man give him a whole dozen of eggs because one of the eggs in the box was cracked. Sometimes the butcher might give him a hunk of unsliced bologna or a few wieners and then maybe the fishman, when he was in a good mood, might give him a catfish or a slice of pickerel or a part of a grass pike.

Every time anybody gives Sandy anything, even if it's just a nickel or a small apple or a handful of gooseberries from the fruit stand, Sandy clicks the heels of his army boots together, stands as straight and tall as he can and gives you the best army salute you ever saw. The salute is so tight that when his fingers reach just above his eyebrow, his whole arm bounces three times just like it's on a spring or something.

Everybody in Ottawa knows about Sandy's salute. And everybody enjoys it when he gives one. And when there's a little crowd like this one in front of the bakery — six or seven people — Sandy makes sure everybody sees the snappy salute and the little crowd laughs and gives Sandy a little bit of happy clapping.

Sandy eats the rest of the piece of chocolate cake the lady in Fenton's Bakery gave him, turns facing the store window, clicks the heels and *Snap* goes the salute!

The show is over.

I go up to him and look down into his squeezed-up face. Even in his big boots, Sandy is short. He must have been the shortest soldier in the war.

"Have you seen Grampa Rip tonight?" I say.

He tells me yes with his face. Sandy doesn't talk.

"Where?"

Sandy turns to go up Somerset Street and then stops and looks back. I follow him up past Borden's Dairy Bar and into the stable.

Half dark in here. Squint to see. We go deeper into the stable and up a ramp. You can hear the horses chewing and sneezing. Sometimes thumping, tails switching against wooden stall walls. The huge stable smells warm and friendly. Brown smell of horse and harness, hay and oats. Sweet horse shit.

Sandy points.

There's Grampa Rip lying down on some bales of hay in one of the empty horse stalls, on his back, peaceful, in his funeral suit, his watch chain glistening, snoring a little bit, a small smile on his lips, a tulip in his buttonhole, his open hand on his head.

The horse in the next stall says something in his throat to say hello to us. Grampa's eyes open.

"I love the smell of horses," he says. "Don't you, whoever you are?"

"It's me, Martin, Grampa Rip. Sandy showed me where you went to. It's time to go home."

"I've had many different jobs in my lifetime, boys. I've been a ditch digger, a paver, a caddy, a door-to-door watch salesman, a tugboat cook, a stonemason, a roofer, a bricklayer, a lumberjack, a log boomer, a pig slaughterer, a manure spreader, a harness maker, an elevator man, a boxcar loader, a railroad man, a bottle washer, a farmer, a mailman, a dynamiter, a sewer worker, a teamster and many, many more... I've seen it all. One of the jobs I had for a while was milkman for Borden's Dairy, years and years ago. My horse's name was Strawberry, one of the first berries of spring. Strawberry knew my milk route as well as I did. I remember, on hot days, she liked me to put a chunk of ice in her mouth to cool her off. I came looking for her tonight.

"She knew every house and store to stop at. You didn't have to tell her. You didn't even have to pick up the reins to steer her. And if there was a sign in the window — NO MILK TODAY, THANK YOU — she wouldn't stop. She'd go on to the next. I swear she could read the signs. Yessir! And between stops I'd read and read my books!"

"Time to come home, Grampa."

"You know, boys, in the old days," says Grampa Rip, "in spring in the Ottawa Valley we had contests, games, cross-cut sawing, rip sawing, needle threading, big picnics, everybody there, potato peeling, pancake eating, eggs boiled in maple syrup...pour maple syrup on everything, on each other, pour maple syrup all over the boys and girls and we bathed ourselves in the sacred dew of the maple tree..."

"Time to come home, Grampa Rip."

Sandy and I help him up and brush the straw off his suit.

"Home?" says Grampa. "Get my horse, Strawberry. She knows the way. Strawberry, my old loyal horse. Take us straight home, no questions asked."

There's a warm spring rain touching tender our faces. We walk the short way home.

At the apartment door Sandy gives us a special salute. We go in. Grampa gets in his chair and I get five dimes out of the Grampa-is-lost bowl.

I go out in the hallway and shut the door. I want to give Sandy the five dimes and I want to talk to him about an idea I have. An idea about "distract, then act." Sandy doesn't talk but I only have to explain the plan to him once and he gets it right away. He'll be there. His nodding tells me that.

Oh, Gerty. Tomorrow I'm comin' to see you with a plan! And tonight, in my sleepiness, I'll go to sleep with you!

16

The Plan

RANDY IS in a good mood today. Today is Saturday. Today is payday. The weather is beautiful. The tulips are all over the place. He's already stolen, with my help, twelve dollars from the first stop we made today at the Parliamentary Restaurant.

"They're easy on Parliament Hill. They just don't seem to pay attention to anything. You could steal the flag off the Peace Tower up there and I bet they wouldn't even notice!"

I'm hoping to get him off his usual subject before he even starts so I tell him that Gerty and I went to see the Marx Brothers movies at the Rialto last week.

"Marx Brothers. Jews. Karl Marx, the inventor of Communism, was their great-grandfather. Those Marx Brothers, they're not funny. No Jews are funny. Oh yeah, maybe they'll try to make you laugh while they're picking your pocket. That's why they get to be comedians.

"The Jews started the First World War and the Second

World War...and now the Commies...did you know...
you know what fluoridization is? No, you probably don't.
Fluoridization is a plan that they're talking about to put
stuff in our drinking water that's supposed to stop your
teeth from rotting. Well, those Commies up there in city
hall, most of them Jews are plotting to poison us all and
take over the city...did you know that Doris Day is a Jew,
her real name is Doris Von Krapelhead or some stupid
thing. Come on, kid. Wake up!"

Randy seems crazier today than usual.

Is it because he's in such a good mood?

While Randy's raving away about Commies and Jews,
I'm thinking about last night. Gerty and I went walking.
The more we walked, the more I told her of my plan. First
I told her some, then more, then all and the more I told
the happier she got. She cried, and then she laughed and
as Randy might say while she laughed the tears rolled
down her eyes. Then she sighed and then her eyes were on
fire, set on fire, flashing with disgust and hatred for Randy.

It was a long walk because I had to tell her about Igor
Gouzenko and the stolen papers and go over the plan with
her again and again.

Gerty likes the plan. She loves the plan. She'll have the
tulips ready. She'll have the back garage unlocked. She
can't wait. She's more excited than I am.

This is Saturday. The last day I'll ever work at Pure
Spring. Randy doesn't know this. He won't know it until
it's too late.

And Randy will never, ever know this.

Last night, in the half-moon light by Baron Strathcona's fountain, I kissed Gerty McDowell on the lips.

We pull up in front of McDowell's Grocery and Lunch on Sweetland.

Gerty is in the doorway of the store. Everything is written on her face that only I can see.

"There's Gerty McDowell," I say. I have put cheerfulness in my voice.

"So *that's* Gerty McDowell! Oh ho! I get it now, Boy. She's your girl! Why didn't you tell me? Hey, she's a nice lookin' piece. Wow wow wow! Way to go, there, Boy O'Boy! Look at the great hair. And the blue ribbon in the hair! Nice touch, there, Romeo. Eh? Eh? You gotta tell me all about her. What she's like, ya know what I'm sayin'?"

We get out of the truck.

"I'll go down. Check the basement," I say.

"Okay," says Randy. "Mind if I have a little chat with your sweetie?"

Instead, there's Sandy coming out of the store just like we planned and he starts a little show for Randy. Gerty gives Sandy a sandwich. He bows. He turns. He begins to eat the sandwich. He salutes.

I'm in the store and down into the cellar. I open the cellar window and crawl out. I can hear Sandy's clicking heels. Now Gerty's giving him the cup of tea. Now the show starts over. More Sandy. More heels clicking.

I pull three full cases of Honee Orange off the truck, careful, no noise, and wheel them into McDowell's garage.

I come back. Now I hear Gerty's voice. Sandy's act is over. Gerty has applauded and got Randy to applaud a bit, too. Gerty is saying, "Mr. Randy, could you come in a minute? I'd like to talk personally to you..." Just like we planned. Distract. Then act!

I pull three more cases, ginger ale this time, off the truck and dolly them into the garage and shut the door. I bring back the dolly, load it quiet, crawl back into the cellar.

Mutt McDowell's stolen cases are back! I'm a thief again, in reverse!

When I come up through the trap door in the store I see Gerty giving Randy the bunch of tulips. Randy loves tulips. I told her about that.

"Oh, *really?*" she said when I told her, her eyes smiling.

"Martin tells me that you've been very kind to him and he arranged that I give you these tulips to give to your lovely wife. He's told me so much about the two of you..." says Gerty.

Randy can't keep his eyes off Gerty. And the tulips. I want to smash Randy's head open with something, anything. Maybe a case of Pure Spring Honee Orange.

"They don't need anything today," I say to Randy. "They've got plenty."

Randy glares at me for a second. Don't *need* anything? What's going on?

Mr. McDowell shuffles out and stands by the cellar window. He's coughing and spitting up.

"There's four cases of empties," I say. "Should I put them out?"

"Might as well," says Randy. He's sniffing the tulips and looking Gerty over.

I go down and pitch out the four cases of empties. I can see Mutt McDowell's skinny legs and his cane tip through the window.

It's over. Distract, then act!

I'm so excited I can hardly breathe. Mr. Mutt McDowell's got back the cases of drinks we stole.

We're back in the truck. Randy won't miss the missing cases until tonight when he takes the truck back to the bottling plant. That's when he counts. Or sometimes, because it's the weekend, he won't bother until Monday.

Depends. But it doesn't matter. I'll never see him again.

Now Randy's back in the truck.

"Old man McDowell sure got to the window in a hurry..."

"Did he?" I say.

"Do you think he's on to us?"

"I don't know. All I know is they didn't need any drinks. Business isn't very good there, I guess."

"Yeah," says Randy. "I heard ya the first time."

We pull away, Sandy and Gerty waving good-bye.

"Who's that jerky little army guy, anyway? Is he crazy?"

"I don't know," I say. "I've never seen him before in my whole life." Granny said once that sometimes telling a lie can be a whole lot of fun!

I'm so happy I feel like jumping out of the truck right now and running back in to Gerty. But I can't. It's not in the plan.

"Oh yeah," says Randy. "I should tell you before I forget. I invited your little patootie over to my place tomorrow for lunch. She said sure. She'd love to. You and pretty little Gerty. Show up at noon."

Now I'm not happy any more.

Now I'm confused.

His place? A lunch?

What is happening?

What Happened • Five

A *LONG CURVING road through ghost black bare trees, branches clawing at the swirling storm.*

Your father pulled Horrors Leblanc's car around the circular driveway.

Then you and your family walked up the wide walk, wide enough for a car. Then three wide concrete steps. Then four granite steps and between four square slate pillars reaching to a canopy. There were three windows over the doors.

The letters carved in the stone above the two large doors: ONTARIO HOSPITAL SCHOOL.

The building was only two stories high.

Inside, two more doors, then a curved lobby and a starched nurse in white greeted you with a wide smile.

What was that smell? Lysol? Piss? Bleach?

Phil was frozen to the floor. You tried to move him but he wouldn't. Then he began to howl. Howling to the high ceiling of the lobby. Howling echoing down two long, long hallways.

Two men in black suits, white shirts, black bow ties, shiny, shiny black shoes came walking with long strides. A nurse arrived with a wheelchair. Phil was acting the worst you've ever seen him. Froth in his mouth. His face choking purple.

Another nurse came with a needle. The two men with the black bow ties grabbed Phil and took off his coat and sweater. The nurse bared his arm and stuck him with a needle.

They put him limp in the wheelchair. They put straps around him so he wouldn't fall out.

Then the whole group of you started down a long hallway. You couldn't see the end, the hall was so long. You walked and you walked and then you walked some more.

Phil was awake now and calmed down. He seemed to be enjoying the ride. Soothing.

It hardly seemed possible but you were still walking. One of the bow ties said the place had over three miles of hallway connecting all the buildings. He seemed proud of it.

And then, after a long time still walking, the other bow tie said, "...and this is one of the shorter ones." It was a joke about the hallway but nobody laughed.

Then the bow tie pushing Phil in the chair said, "What's his name? You said Phil? Let's speed things up a bit here, Phil!" And he took off running ahead, running ahead pushing Phil down the hallway for the ride of his life until they got smaller and smaller and Phil giggling hysterically — the fun of it!

"Wheeee!" Phil screamed with delight. They became just dots down there where they at last stopped to wait for us. Phil's voice echoing down through the long hall.

Papers signed.

It was time to go.

Your mother tried hugging Phil but he didn't want to.

"That's enough," your father said. "He doesn't understand. You're just making things worse. Let's go."

Standing sad there.

You remembered, for some reason, something that happened a long time ago.

You got on the St. Patrick Street streetcar and your mother was standing with Phil out there on the sidewalk. It was summer and the streetcar windows were open and you waved at Phil as soon as you sat down and you were surprised when you saw Phil wave back. You were sure he did — at least a little bit of a wave. You saw it, you were startled by it — he never waved before — and you felt so glad but your father said afterwards no, Phil was too stupid to wave, he didn't know what waving meant, he couldn't have waved, he was probably swatting a fly or scratching his head or something, but you thought he waved because he looked right at you and his hand went up and it was a nice look he had on his face that you'd never seen before...

Time to go.

"Phil," you said. Phil looked up from the ice cream that they gave him. You waved. "Bye, Phil," you said.

Phil looked.

Your twin looked at you.

Strange eyes not yours.

Did he wave?

Or was he just going back at the ice cream with his spoon?

Time to go.

Time to go.

Go.

Leave Phil there. Bye bye.

17

Running Away with Gerty

GERTY WANTS to get him. Get Randy. There's a fire in her that scares me. She doesn't seem to be afraid of anything.

We'll go. We agree. Gerty says we'll go. Go to Randy's. We won't stay long. Just long enough to steal the papers for Igor and then out the door we go. What could be wrong with that? Just go in. Wait for a chance to steal the papers for Igor. Then out we go. Run. What can he do? We'll never see Randy again.

Gerty, I think, is more brave than I am. But I want to be the brave one.

"We'll do it. We'll go. We'll fix Randy twice this way," I say bravely. Her fire makes me so excited.

This is the girl I love. She always surprises, there's always surprises in her! Spring surprises. Gerty surprises.

We walk over from Sandy Hill to Lowertown to number 60 Cobourg Street. We have umbrellas. It's a big springtime rain. A warm kissing rain. Dark day. Even though it's noon, it's like evening. Everything is soft. Pussy-willow soft. The spring rain closes us in. It's like a private cave in the rain that is nobody else's but ours. The rain is a room. Our own room.

We look up at the red brick building with the dirty streaked-down windows like people have been crying on them.

Inside, we go up the shaky elevator.

We knock and Randy opens the door. The apartment has no lights on. Candles on the kitchen table.

"Welcome. Welcome to lunch. My wife can't make it. Have a seat at the kitchen table. Be careful of the candles. Don't set fire to yourselves."

He leaves. He sounds happy as anything. Randy sounds happy but I know he's pretending. He's not happy, he's angry. I know him. I know his angry voice.

I take a peek into the darkened living room.

Nobody there.

I go in. Look up at the dirty book shelf filled with old newspapers and magazines. There's the dusty stopped clock. There's the folder. The folder with Igor's pages in Russian.

I grab it and slip back into the kitchen. I show it to Gerty. She's looking around to find a place to hide it. I take it and shove it under my shirt. It shows. He'll see. Gerty pulls the curtain of the kitchen window aside and lets the light into the gloom. The kitchen window is open about half way. There's a bit of breeze. She tries to open it more. It won't go. There's a big nail holding it there.

We hear Randy coming back. Gerty takes the folder. She lifts her dress away up and slides the folder down inside her blue panties with the pink ribbon trim. Then she drops her dress and with both hands smooths the front down.

We can hear Randy's footsteps coming.

I try the kitchen door. Locked. No key.

He comes into the gloomy kitchen and sits at the table. He's got a big knife. He rams it hard into the table. It stands quivering there.

"Now," says Randy. "Last night, when I did my inventory, I noticed I'm missing six cases, full. Three ginger, three Honee. I figure you two crooks took these cases from Randy's truck yesterday while we were admiring the tulips...right? Randy doesn't like crooks. Nobody steals from Randy and gets away with it."

While he's talking, he's looking at the knife sticking in the table. But I'm looking at him. And while I'm looking at him I have a strange feeling that I'm getting bigger. For the first time, I realize that I'm bigger than Randy.

Ever since what happened I've felt so small, like I was disappearing, but now Randy looks like such a pipsqueak compared to me.

Randy pulls the knife out of the wooden table and drives it back in. Making a frightening noise.

"So now, your punishment. Boy, tell your little patootie here to start taking off her clothes. Give old Randy a little payback for getting robbed! Know what I mean?"

Time to get out of here.

I stand up and lift the table up over on top of Randy and as he hits the floor, I pick up the chair I was sitting on and bring it smashing down on top of him. Then I turn and smash the window out with the chair.

"Out the window!" I yell at Gerty, and when she's half way out the window I go back and smash Randy down with the chair again.

I'm tearing at the curtain and shoving Gerty out through the opening over the broken glass onto the fire escape. The glass is cutting us and there's blood.

And I look back while I'm crawling out after her and there's Randy with the big knife stabbing at me and missing my legs and I tumble out on to the fire escape, the taste of black iron in my mouth.

I race after Gerty down the bouncing squeaking shaking metal stairs. Up above, out the window, Randy is screeching, "Come back here yez little snot-nosed crook criminals. Stole six cases from my truck. Police! Police! Randy's going to kill you, Boy! Wait and see! Nobody steals from Randy!"

It's almost like when Mr. George was screaming at Billy Batson and me when we ruined his organ concert back then at St. Alban's Church.

Gerty is wild-eyed and so am I.

We feel as in a dream.

We're running so beautiful. Striding together. I'm surprised how fast Gerty can run, as we run streaking through the warm rain, blood flying off our cuts from the broken window.

"The papers," I say. "Igor's papers. Have you got them?"

"They're right here," she says, running and panting. "Safe and sound right here," she says, patting her belly.

And I'm safe and sound, too.

Bigger than I ever felt.

18

Goodbye, Mr. Mirsky

IT'S 10:00 A.M. in the morning here at Pure Spring Bottling Company, 22 Aberdeen Street. It rained early in the morning and the streets are clean and fresh. There's a nice breeze, warm in the cool, and there's a smell of flowers and breakfast toast in the air. Birds are chirping and nesting.

Anita is in her office and I don't have to wait very long to get to see her.

"Right choo are, Martin O'Boy!" she says. "Glad to see you. What do ya think?"

"I think Randy is a thief," I say. And then I say, "And so am I."

Anita's eyelashes do a few nervous ups and downs.

"And I want to tell Mr. Mirsky," I say. "My Grampa Rip says tell it all and it will all go away."

"Hold on there, hold on there, my boy. Let's not get ahead of ourselves. Start telling me first where you got all the cuts on your hands and your arms. And those two on your face. Your forehead. And your cheek."

"Randy invited my friend Gerty and me over to his place for lunch yesterday with him and his wife but his wife wasn't there and he took out a knife and he wanted me to tell my friend Gerty to take off her clothes so I hit him with a chair and then I broke the window and we escaped."

"You hit Randy with a chair?"

"Yes. Twice."

The air in the room isn't moving. Nothing is moving. Anita's eyelashes aren't moving. The frills on her blouse aren't moving. Her bracelets aren't moving. Even her perfume is still.

"First of all," says Anita, "your Randy has no wife. Your Randy's wife ran away two years ago with another man. One of the other drivers. Can you blame her? Married to a nut like that? Guy named Freeman. Irish guy. Randy thought it was Freiman like the department store, A.J. Freiman. So Randy figured Freeman was Jewish. Told everybody all the time how he hated Jews."

I take out my list of thievery and put it on the desk.

"Before I show you this I have to tell you something. I lied to Mr. Mirsky about my age. I'm not sixteen. I won't be sixteen until August 6, the day they dropped the bomb. I'm only fifteen."

"You could pass for eighteen. You would've gotten away with it."

"I couldn't stop thinking about it."

"Conscience."

"And then I helped Randy steal from the customers. Here's every cent we stole and how we stole it on this list."

Anita looks over the list.

Then her phone buzzes.

She answers.

"Right choo are, Mr. Mirsky," she says and gets up.

"You come back in one hour," she says. "And take a seat outside Mr. Mirsky's office. Wait there. I'll get your pay ready. He'll probably want to talk to you. In fact, I know he will."

* * *

"This is quite the document, Martin O'Boy. Quite the document indeed."

Mr. Mirsky is not behind his desk. He's sitting beside me on the sofa that's there in his office for special visitors.

"All of these customers will have to be apologized to and reimbursed."

"Not all."

"Oh?"

"McDowell's Grocery and Lunch has already been apologized to. And reimbursed."

"Oh?" (Reimbursed: a new word to show Grampa Rip.)

"Yes."

"I see. Knowing you as I do, I believe there's an interesting story there."

"Yes, sir."

"And this document, as I was saying. Very effective. And excellently written, I might add. The description of each crime. Very clear, graphic. You have a very fine style."

"Thank you."

"You know, of course, you'll have to resign."

"Yes, I know."

"We'll deal with Randy. He needs a lot of help. Psychological help."

I'm looking at Mr. Mirsky and he's looking at me. There's understanding in his face.

"This has been a trying and dangerous time for you. But you came through it with flying colors, as they say."

I look at him, frowning a bit.

"Flying colors? It's a military term. A fleet of ships returns to port victorious in battle, all their flags flying in celebration."

I don't know what to say.

"When you turn sixteen you can come back and we'll hire you immediately. But I'd rather see you going to school. Bright boy like you. Get your education."

Mr. Mirsky hands me a small brown envelope.

"Your pay. You'll find some extra in there. Let's call it an integrity bonus."

"Thank you, sir."

"I'm going to visit each and every one of these customers personally and see to it that they are reimbursed.

And I want you to come with me as a reliable witness. Will you do that for me?"

"Yes, sir. I will."

"Anita will notify you."

"Yes, sir."

"You never did tell us everything that happened."

"Maybe I will some day."

"Good-bye, Martin O'Boy."

"Good-bye, Mr. Mirsky."

What Happened • Six

YOU WERE heading home. Your father had another bottle. Where did he get them all? Sipping from it, talking about the future of your family.

"Everything's going to be different. We're going to have a normal family from now on. And there'll be no more drinkin'. No more booze. Soon's I finish this bottle, get home, sleep it all off — be a new man, a new morning! What d'ya think of that?"

"I'll believe it when I see it," your mother said, only whispering.

The snow seemed to make the car so quiet.

"And we'll have to get rid of that cat of yours," he said over his shoulder to you in the backseat. "Have him put down. It doesn't hurt. You use chloroform. You know there was cat hair in my coffee the other day? And on my toothbrush one time? I must have been drunk or something that day. Buying an old scruffy cat like that..."

Did Cheap know he was alive? you thought. Did he

know he could die? Somebody could have him killed? Did he wonder if anybody loved him? Did he care? Cheap, he could be strangled, murdered tonight, now. Nobody would stand up and say this is wrong. Who protects Cheap except you? You're in charge of his life. If he lives or dies it's up to you.

And Phil? Who cares for Phil now?

THE TRIAL. You are accused of the heinous crime of not caring for your twin brother Phil...

You lay down on the backseat. Rest. Tired, maybe sleep. You would go later and see Phil sometime, you guessed. He looked at you. His eyes said he'd see you soon, you thought. Maybe he even waved.

The snow was driving straight into the windshield. You could get hypnotized. Watching the snowflakes come hurtling straight at you out of the dark, out of nowhere. You could start to imagine you were diving down, not speeding forward but down, down, a no-bottom hole right through the planet earth and out the underside and deep, deeper into outer space and the snowflakes glittering in the headlights of Horrors Leblanc's car and there were stars whizzing past in a galaxy like a long hallway as you dove, dove deeper into the nowhere faster than light goes...

And in your dream you were hurtling through space with Phil and Phil was laughing and singing and he knew all the words and how smart he was all of a sudden.

"Wheeee!" Phil screamed with delight!

Phil was singing just like Dorothy in The Wizard of Oz *singing, "Birds fly over the rainbow..."*

Phil, smarter even than you, Martin, smarter than you!

Phil, happy, singing his little heart out, laughing at the whizzing stars, "Why then oh why can't I?"

And now there was a Bang...Bang...Bang... *and a shaking and a screaming of metal and glass.*

And there was silence. Then a hissing sound.

And you were buried alive in the dark there for a long time — maybe you were still asleep, you thought and then sirens and car doors slamming and voices and then a light shining and then another and another.

And you were wedged in down on the floor and facing up and one of the lights showed you something sitting in the corner of the backseat.

Snowflakes coming in. Where was the roof of Horrors Leblanc's car? He was going to be very disappointed by what you'd done to his new car.

They got you out and in the ambulance.

Out the window you saw them uncover something in the snowbank. The light shone on it. They put it in a sack.

Your mother's body was still in the front seat of the car with your father's.

When you started feeling bigger, Grampa Rip and you talked about flat-bed trucks. Empty flat-bed trucks. If you run into the back of a parked flat-bed truck that has *no load on, the flat-bed of the truck acts like a large horizontal knife and it comes right through the front window, shaving off the top of the car and also the heads of people sitting up in the front seat.*

Your head is like a heavy ball sitting on your shoulders, attached only by a few skinny muscles, some flimsy bones and some veins.

You could knock a person's head off with a baseball bat if you hit it right, the same as you could knock a small pumpkin off a gatepost.

Grampa Rip told you that when his friend Mutt McDowell was in the First World War he was running toward the enemy and the soldier running along beside him got his head knocked off his body by a shell and the soldier ran, kept running for more than a few steps before he fell over.

You were almost well enough then to talk about it but not for very long.

You had felt so small for so long.

19

Big Now

SOMETIMES I pinch Cheap's skin and fur at the back
of his neck — pull on it a bit like I guess his mother
must have done to carry him around when he was little
before he was taken away from her and shoved in a pet
store window and sold for ten cents as a joke because he
only had one ear.

When I do this with Cheap he closes his eyes and turns
toward me and looks up at me and goes all soft like he
wants me to kiss him.

I've showed this to Gerty. We laughed about it. She
asked me to try it with her.

Now I'm trying it with her on the park bench right
next to the Gray Man's park bench.

A couple of weeks ago, Grampa Rip wrote to "Mr. John
Smith" and soon after, Igor Gouzenko showed up, got his
papers, told us he'd been offered five thousand dollars for
the complete package, promised he'd send us a ten percent
bonus. That night we had a party — Gerty and I found

Sandy and brought him — and Igor was happy and tried to teach us a Russian dance. Sandy was the funniest trying it.

Grampa Rip wanted to invite the Gray Man, but one peek out the round window and we knew he was off duty. Igor told us he wasn't worried about the Gray Man.

"He is no danger to me now," said Igor. "His heart is not in it any more. Soon he, too, will defect to Canada."

Then Igor asked Grampa Rip what was locked in his big strongbox that was so heavy.

Everybody helped pull the box out into the living room and gathered round while he turned the key in the big padlock.

Full of pennies, nickels and dimes!

Just like the great-grandaddy of the bowl on the hall table.

"For a rainy day," said Grampa Rip, and he cried a little bit. "Been saving it almost all my life! For a rainy day. And no rainy day yet!" We picked up handfuls of the coins and ran them through our fingers. Grampa Rip gave two fistfuls of them for Sandy's pockets.

"Some of it will come in handy for Martin to go back to school," says Grampa Rip, putting his arm around my shoulders.

It was, Gerty said, the best party she was ever at.

And I said I agree with you, my sweetheart.

It's 4:00 P.M. in the afternoon on a lilac-and-tulip day in the slanting sun.

Billy Finbarr, the paper boy, is watching us while he's folding up his biscuits to throw at the houses.

The Gray Man is sidespying us, too.

There are two squirrels in the maple tree above us, watching. A couple of pigeons, eyes like buttons, are watching.

There's Sandy on his rounds, marching across the park. He sees, too.

There's Grampa Rip coming up the street in his funeral wake clothes, now turning into the apartment, his back and shoulders looking happy. He waves and sees, too.

I pinch the nape of Gerty's neck right where the hairline grows in downy wisps. Like a little kitty she laughs and purrs on purpose and turns toward me and looks up at me, imitating Cheap, and goes all soft, like she wants me to...kiss her...

But I can't. Too many eyes looking. Even Smitty outside Smitty's Smoke Shop is standing outside his shop, looking across at us in the park.

And everybody on the streetcar that is rumbling by, even the driver, is looking at us. And the priest standing on the porch of St. Elijah's Antiochian Orthodox Church looking up from his book is looking at us.

Billy Finbarr, paperboy, comes across the street to our bench.

"Hey, Billy," I say. "What's on the front page today?"

"First day of summer!" says Billy Finbarr to me, but he's looking at Gerty. "I've seen you before," says Billy.

"This is Gerty McDowell, Billy," I say, trying to get rid of him.

"Hubba! Hubba!" says Billy, moving his eyebrows up and down like Groucho Marx does in the movies.

"Cut it out, Billy!" I say. "You're too young for that, ya little shrimp."

"Not too young to know," says Billy, stealing from Nat "King" Cole's song.

Gerty laughs, her skin like white roses brushed in pink.

"If you ever need anything, Gerty, I live right over there — 337 Lyon Street, two doors from the church, second floor. See the balcony?" says Billy, making his eyebrows jump again.

"I see it, Billy Finbarr," Gerty says, and then gives him a smile that makes me mad enough to go and shove Billy head first down the nearest storm sewer.

"Scram, Billy," I say, but not mean, more friendly.

After a while Gerty puts her head on my shoulder.

"The Gray Man," she says in my ear. "I wonder how long he's going to sit there?"

"Probably forever," I say, talking too loud on purpose. "I wonder if he is stupid like Igor said."

I'm pinching Gerty's nape, my eyes half closed, when I feel a shadow over us.

The Gray Man stands blocking the glancing sun from the west. He's very tall, has large hands and a chest like a big wall. He has a low voice. He has hardly any Russian accent.

"Not stupid," he says. "Not stupid at all. How's your friend Igor doing? I saw him, you know. Don't worry, I won't report it. Soon I'll join him. As a Canadian citizen,

I mean. You young people think you know everything. You don't know how lucky you are. You don't realize that to be born in Canada at this present time in history is the greatest gift that can be thrust upon any person on this planet. I'd think very seriously about that, if I were you."

He leaves, strides away down Somerset Street, doesn't look back, disappears.

Time to walk. Gerty takes my hand. We walk across Dundonald Park and into the summer that's starting. I'm getting to feel pretty big right now. Not disappearing like I was.

"Do you think we will be together always, Martin?" she asks.

"I don't know, Gerty," I say. "I don't know about that. Guy like me, the way I am. All I know about is today."

"I think we will," says Gerty.

And our clasped hands clasp tighter.

"Will you come with me to visit my twin brother Phil where he's at? We'll take the bus?"

"Oh, yes, I will," she says. "Yes, I will. I'll go anywhere with you."

This is all I can say. I'm afraid to say more. I'll die if I say more.

The lilac trees, smelling like deep lilac, hang over us as we walk.

Die of happiness.

Dramatis Personae

Martin O'Boy - he felt so small he almost disappeared,
but he got big again because of Love
Mr. Mirsky - a kind, good man
Granny - her advice stays with Martin
Grampa Rip Sawyer - much more than just a grampa
Cheap - a loyal one-eared companion
Buz Sawyer - off to be a war hero, again
Father - a piece of work
Phil - the damaged twin
Mother - the one who suffered
Smitty - he's part of the Gray Man's scenery
Anita - short perfumed tornado
Billy Batson - an old friend, gone
Fred MacMurray - he looks just like Captain Marvel
except for his clothes
Virgin Mary - a beautiful lady in blue
Jesus - her son
The Mud Pout - an ugly woman

Frankie and Johnny - they'll handle your valuables
Hack Sawyer - an old-time genius
Mr. Applebaum - a religious bigot
Dundonald - somebody they named a park after
Billy Finbarr - a flirtatious paper boy
The Gray Man - a "surveyor"
Esther Williams - long legs and a bathing suit
Randy - a guy whose brainpan needs to be hosed out
    with industrial-strength disinfectant
Mutt McDowell - an unfortunate, unsung, coughing war
    hero
Gerty McDowell - she's so...
Nat "King" Cole - he sings the word "love" just right
Dermit - an old pal from sixty years ago
Kelly O'Kelly - the world's oldest usher
Pete Lowell - a legendary streetcar conductor
Horrors Leblanc - he used to have a brand-new car
Igor Gouzenko - a Canadian hero/Russian traitor
Habitant pea soup - a biceps builder
Shipper - likes looking at "wedding" pictures
McEvoy's - a good place to visit — if you're still alive
Sandy - he gets around town
Matuta - a morning person
Red Skelton - a clown
Mrs. Laflamme - a former neighbor with many children
Mrs. Sawyer - she knows the neighbors' business
Horseball Laflamme - an old friend with a not-very-nice
    first name
Mr. Lachaine - he owns Lachaine's, a store

Karl Marx - he never worked at Pure Spring
Tony Bennett - he can make your life worthwhile
James Joyce - a famous writer
Ulysses - gets lost trying to get home
Waitress at Bellamy's - experienced in damaged children
Two Carleton Place locals - weather experts
Prime Minister St. Laurent - a gentleman
Strawberry - a workhorse who can read
Doris Day - she could sing your heart out
Two men with bow ties - they take Phil for a long ride
Dorothy - she wants to fly like the bluebirds
The Soldier - he lost his head

Author's Note

OTTAWA VALLEY people for generations have had affection for and fond memories of Pure Spring soft drinks. An Ottawa original in style and taste, the company was founded by David Mirsky in the 1920s. He started with water bubbling out of the limestone cliff at Bronson and Wellington streets known as Nanny Goat Hill. Pure spring water it was, hence the company name.

Honee Orange, Swiss Cream Soda, Grapefruit 'N Lime, Gini, Uptown and, of course, ginger ale are some of the dozen or more flavors we all came to crave.

The community-minded Mirsky family ran an honest, unpretentious business serving the mighty and the humble, the embassy and the corner confectioner with equal aplomb.

Many with memory in the region can still taste the Honee Orange sliding smooth down the throat on an endless, full-of-promise, hot spring day.

The final batch of Pure Spring colors was bottled locally in the 1990s.

We salute the Mirsky family and extend heartfelt thanks to Paul and Peter Mirsky for sharing their personal memorabilia.

PURE SPRING
1911 - 1995

Acknowledgments

The following sources were invaluable to me in the gathering of this tale.

Rick Brown
Mike Doyle
Dave Dunlap
Sandy Farquharson
Bob Gairns
A. E. Housman
James Joyce
Marilyn Kennedy
Lenny Marcus
William G. D. McCarthy
Paul Mirsky
Peter Mirsky
Paddy Mitchell
Sandy Morris
Joyce Carol Oates
Mike Paradis
Jay Roberts
Terry West
Peter Worthington